Kram Kollection

Kram Rednip

FIRST EDITION
Published in 2023 by
Green Cat Books
19 St Christopher's Way
Pride Park
Derby
DE24 8JY

www.green-cat.shop

ISBN: 978-1-913794-58-3

DEDICATION

This book is dedicated to all my Ukrainian friends and former colleagues. Thinking of the jolly times we had together in Kyiv in 2016-2018, and hoping that for all of you the future will bring much, much better things than right now.

CONTENTS

ACKNOWLEDGEMENTS

Inspiration for the Kollection has come from two writers of comic fiction greatly admired by the author – Robert Smith Surtees and Hector Hugh Munro ('Saki'). Kram has frequently tried, but usually failed, to capture the essence of their creative genius in his own scribblings.

Acknowledgements also of the patience of family members who have, at various times, critiqued these stories (not always favourably!). Also the editorial and production work of the team at Green Cat Books, who have persevered mightily in the face of Kram's petty insistences concerning use of capitals, punctuation, text alignment etc. in preparing the Kollection for print.

Gary United

1. The Grand Scheme: 2000-2002

Football fever was sweeping the country - sweeping the whole world, even, it seemed. The 20th World Cup, held in France the previous summer, had been a resounding success - even the French were still talking about it. Superstar players, superstar coaches, some of them bigger than the game itself, seemingly - all, all riding high on a tidal wave of euphoria, astronomical transfer fees, astronomical salaries, new greenfield site, all-weather stadia. 'Are Manchester United bigger than God?' screamed out one tabloid headline - the Archbishop of Canterbury was outraged, to the merriment of the football crazy, football daft *hoi polloi*.

*****

Although he came from Manchester, Jack Openshaw had never been a big Manchester United fan. To put it plainly, he resented their success. Nevertheless, he settled down in his hotel room at the Karachi Marriott after a hard day's deal-making, to watch their European Cup Final game against Bayern Munich.

Watching football matches on satellite television was a little comfort Jack always allowed himself when away from home on business. Karachi was a particularly tough destination for him, since Pakistan was a dry country and, in theory at least, he couldn't obtain an alcoholic drink. No G and T, no B and S; all that was available at the Marriott were a few 33 cl. cans of fizzy, sickly lager, and even getting your hands on these demanded an elaborate ceremony involving presentation of your passport at the reception desk, and signed declarations that you were a non-Muslim, would not take the stuff away from the hotel premises, etc.

'Five bloody dollars! Bloody liberty, the price they demand for this stuff...' Jack grumbled to himself, wiping his lips in distaste as he sucked the first metallic-tasting mouthful out of the can and settled down to watch the game. Painstakingly extending his heavy frame across the bed in his hotel room, he twiddled with the air-conditioning controls until he got the temperature just right. Then, reaching for the remote control, he flipped through the TV channels until finding the one broadcasting the game.

'Oh no! Bloody Yank commentators!'

It was an American sports network, fresh and enthusiastic, but not for the connoisseur. This and the cloying aftertaste of the lager combined to put Jack in a bad mood.

'They just don't bleedin' well know what they're talkin' about. Should stick to baseball, or that other bloody incomprehensible rubbish - Yank football.'

He turned the sound down, so he could watch the little human figures of the players scurrying about from left to right, from right to left across the television screen in peace. He took some satisfaction from the fact that Manchester United were losing one-nil, and were not playing well. But he still wasn't really enjoying himself. He was very tired, and a few minutes before the end of the game, he yawned, flicked the television off and went to sleep.

*****

Murray Alexander-Walker, Jack's personal assistant, called him on his mobile as he was taking breakfast the next morning.

'How's it been? Oh, the usual stuff - the Trade and Industry boys want their piece of the action on the quiet - but I think the deal'll go through all right. I'll hand over the files to Raschid, in the local office this afternoon. He can handle it OK from now on. Then I'm coming home. Book me onto a flight ... oh, tomorrow morning, can you?'

Scooping a couple of forkfuls of scrambled egg into his mouth, Jack tried to catch what Murray was saying - his voice was breaking up on the crackly line.

'What's that? How's Karachi? Oh, it's all right. Climate's fucking awful, of course, so bloody humid, my glasses steam up every time I step into the lobby. And the hotel's crap, room too small, very cramped. The walls are too thin.'

In fact, despite all the minor irritations, Jack rather enjoyed coming to Karachi. He liked to have a moan, and as long as you could handle their way of doing things, all the bribery and backhanders and that stuff, all his deals always went through OK. The local office managers were reliable enough, they could handle those things properly. As for the hotel room - well, it was his own choice to stay in a standard room - after all, he was rich enough to buy up the whole hotel, and all the others in Karachi, if he wanted to. He just didn't like unnecessary expense.

'Just book me on economy class, will you? And there's one

other thing, Murray - you know - the game - the lads?'

'The what? Oh, you mean Hensthorpe Athletic? Not too good, I'm afraid. Went down again - four-nil.'

'Four-nil? So, that's it then. They're going down. Oh, Bloody Nora, the Unibond bloody League, division two, next season then.'

'Never mind, Jack, never mind. Did you see the big game last night? Marvellous finish. Looked like they weren't going to do it, but they did in the end.'

'What d'you mean? One-nil, wasn't it?'

'Yes it was, until injury time. Then they got two goals right at the end, both in the last two minutes. Solskjær and Sheringham. Marvellous finish.'

'Oh, Bloody Nora...'

Miserably, Jack switched off his mobile phone. Manchester United winning like that was bad enough, but Hensthorpe Athletic! He was chairman of the club, after all, he'd never live this down back home in Cheadle Hulme. At Rotary Club meetings, out on the golf course... it was too bad to be true.

*****

Jack couldn't remember how he had ever come to be Chairman of Hensthorpe Athletic Association Football Club (founded: 1926). It had been at one of those Rotary Club meetings - he must've had one or two too many G and Ts, the local MP or some other silly bugger had proposed him, and that was that. As the most prominent businessman in North-East Cheshire, he could hardly have refused, after all. So he had taken the job on, not really expecting or being expected to do more than fork out the occasional thousand quid or so to cover travelling expenses, the new first team away strip, or whatever.

It was his wife who first noticed the difference in him. When she told him, he was flabbergasted; he couldn't explain it to himself, let alone to her. But the fact was, he had become passionate about the club. Not that it made much difference, at first. Jack was too diffident to get involved - too shy of poking his nose in where he thought it might not be wanted, being seen as an amateur blundering about amongst the semi-professionals. He still agreed with all the questionable decisions made by the manager - Colin Allardyce, formerly of Sheffield United reserves and Hartlepool United - and watched in dismay as the team slid hopelessly down into the lower regions of the Unibond League (Premier Division). Occasionally, he would stump up a few thousand quid more for some new player - generally a crony of Allardyce's, some one-time hopeful professional seeking a safety net after dropping out of the bottom of the Nationwide League.

Jack was not a reflective man, but if he had been, he might have thought long and hard about what it was to be a football fanatic. Why, in God's name, did he care? What made him so miserable for days afterwards, when the team lost yet again? Until a couple of years before he had never even heard of Hensthorpe Athletic - now here he was, having just concluded a business deal involving almost half the raw cotton fibre production in Sindh Province, and all he wanted to know about was - the result of last night's game, not the Big One in Barcelona, the Other One. Another surrender in the rain at the Nailmaker's Row Ground, watched by the coach, the assistant coach, the groundsman and one or two old gaffers who remembered the club's glory days of the 1920s and '30s when promotion to the old Third Division (North) had been almost a possibility; and then, knowing the result, being so depressed about it. He just couldn't rationalise it. He was angry with himself, so angry, for being so stupid and miserable. But try as he might, he couldn't break free from it.

*****

Jack never knew, either, if it was his wife who told Murray Alexander-Walker about his secret passion, or whether somehow Murray just found out by himself. But it was following his return from that trip to Karachi - Murray must have noticed how down in the dumps he was, despite the success of the venture - that he broached The Subject.

'Listen, Jack. I've had a thought about something. It might seem a bit way-out to you at first. But I've really given it a lot of thought, and I'm convinced it could work.'

'Oh yeah? Something to do with, what d'you call it, 'worldwide branding' or summat? Most of your bright ideas are. Well, spit it out then, lad.'

Jack got on well with Murray, somehow thinking of him as the son he never had, but with his advertising agency background he was always suspicious of his clever, creative ideas for expanding the business even further. After all, marketing wasn't making things, it was just clever, clever stuff that somehow could boost the bottom line almost overnight, it seemed, without you having to do very much. Except you always had to spend a right lot of money - that was what made Jack suspicious, despite the fact that Murray's grand schemes almost always worked incredibly well.

'It'll cost a lot of money, I s'pose? An' what if it doesn't work? You sure we can afford it?'

'Jack, let me explain. Of course it'll work. And of course we can afford it. The money's absolutely no problem - oh, Jack, have you no idea at all what you and the company are really worth?'

Jack didn't know it, but he was in fact the richest man in the United Kingdom - in the whole of Western Europe, probably. He didn't know it, because nobody else knew it (Murray apart) and therefore nobody had ever told him about it. His way of doing business was so cautious, so secretive - a snail's progress over many long years, starting with his first little venture and gradually building it up into a bigger venture, then into two, into three, into lots and lots of different ventures, until it was effectively a huge conglomerate of local monopolies, loosely - and invisibly - controlled by himself and the boy Murray. Thus, he never made it into any of those 'richest 1000 people in Britain' lists put together by the Sunday newspapers every now and then, to boost their circulation figures by tickling up the latent envies of their readers, the professional classes. Jack didn't regard himself as 'professional class'; he never read any newspaper other than the Daily Telegraph, and he never felt spiteful, greedy or envious. Why should he? He had a nice enough house in a nice suburb, a silver-grey Jag to ride about in, a ride-on lawnmower for Sundays. He had a commonsensical wife, who respected his judgement and knew how to get on with things and people at social gatherings. His two daughters, both recently married and with their own careers, were off his hands now. Yes, Jack was a contented, unenvious man - except when it came to Hensthorpe Athletic.

Murray was not usually shy, or unpersuasive in 'spitting out' one of his money-making schemes for the business. For once, however - after coming up with his initial, bold statement - he seemed tongue-tied and just couldn't explain what was on his mind. All Jack could grasp was that it had something to do with Hensthorpe Athletic. In the end, he had to help Murray a little.

'I don't quite see what you're driving at, lad. Some kind of sponsorship thing, is that what it is?'

'Yes... sponsorship, the company logo, advertising hoardings, that sort of thing, yes... that's part of it, certainly...'

'Well, what then? I s'pose we could manage to do something for the lads, you know, have the logo on the front of their shirts and so forth. I s'pose that'd look quite nice. Don't see the benefit to the company, though: it's not exactly in your worldwide branding league, is it?'

'No... no, it isn't...'

They were having their meeting in private in the company boardroom, sitting together at one end of the big, teak-finish conference table. Murray was still having unprecedented difficulty in expressing himself. He looked so awkward, fiddling with his teacup and saucer, knocking the little silver sugar spoon onto the carpet so he had to dive down under the polished surface of the table and fish it up again.

'But, you see, that's only part of what I have in mind. An important part, of course, I'm sure you see that... but it's not the part that's going to cost all the money.'

'So what is, then? Investing in the club, that's what you mean, isn't it? Buying a few new half-decent players. Well, I don't mind that. Not a bad long-term strategy for all concerned. Don't know why I didn't think of it myself. Yeah - with the company name on the front of their shirts, away strip an' all, an' in a few years' time, if maybe we can get back into the First Division, maybe even the Premier Division or the Vauxhall Conference...'

Murray put down his teacup and looked up at Jack suddenly, worriedly. He looked nervous, excited and unsure of himself all at the same time.

'That's about the shape of it, Jack, that's what I've been thinking. It's very simple, really. But what's not so simple about it - which is why it's been so difficult for me to put it across to you - is the scale of what I have in mind. Forget the Vauxhall Conference, Jack, we've got to aim much higher than that. And returning to your very first question: yes, it is going to cost money - a very great deal of money.'

Jack sighed, sat back in the hard-bottomed boardroom chair, and listened to what Murray had to say. It was a new, daring, almost diabolical plan, a plan that only Murray could ever have thought of, and the name of the plan was 'Gary United'.

*****

It is necessary to explain here, that the name which generally identified Jack's loose federation of companies was 'Garrymore Holdings'. The name served no useful purpose other than that it had no obvious association with Jack, and therefore was one tiny filament in the complex web of obscurity that so thoroughly preserved his business anonymity. Jack had deliberately chosen the name himself, for this purpose. It had also been a little whim of his - 25 Garrymore Street, Stockport, Cheshire had been the address of his first ever little venture, a machine shop turning out a new kind of bale arm for weaving equipment that Jack had invented, back in 1963.

Carefully, and deliberately, Murray set out on his explanation. The more he explained, the more daring, fantastic, downright insane the whole scheme of things appeared - and yet, curiously enough, the more he explained, the more Jack started to believe the whole thing might work.

'I've done my research, you see, Jack. I've really, really gone into all the details, in a big way. I didn't want to tell you much about it, I <u>knew</u> I could only begin to convince you if I presented you with the full picture. Of course, there's still all sorts of things we'll have to agree on, before we put together any kind of plan for board approval, and I think most of those things we'll have to work out on our own, Jack.'

'Certainly. I can see that, plainly enough. Strictly for our eyes only, for the time being.'

Murray had warmed to his theme, at last. The old advertising executive's inspirational light of battle was glittering in his eye.

'One final little detail - it's only a detail, but in a sense it's the most important thing of all - the name of the team. We'll have to change the name, straight off. Make it more catchy, more universal, and also more identifiable with the company. So, the team's going to have to be called 'Gary United'.'

Jack's old-fashioned sensibilities - and his loyalty to the club - balked at this at once.

'You what?' he spluttered. 'GARY UNITED?! What kind of a name is that? I mean, why? Is it really necessary? Seems a bit way-out to me. Oh, I see the gist of it, of course, but isn't the current name good enough? Bit more...traditional, I'd have thought, speaking for myself...'

*****

In his younger days in the 1950s, when he had only just started thinking up his schemes for making his millions, Jack had briefly worked as company secretary for a big retail co-operative in Manchester. The experience had helped to form his business mindset, making him cautious, methodical, attentive to detail - the perfect counterweight in many ways, to Murray Alexander-Walker. One of his chief business pleasures even now was setting things down on paper, in a neat, methodical, unambiguous way, like the secretary to a committee or board of directors. Therefore, once Murray had explained his plan to him, he hunted up some sheets of plain foolscap paper and a ballpoint pen from a drawer in the sideboard and started to set down Gary United in plain words, so there could be no misunderstanding about it between Murray and himself.

Jack's minutes of the Grand Scheme read like this:

Item: public relations and sponsorship venture, the two parties to the agreement being first, Garrymore Holdings (UK) Ltd (hereafter referred to as 'the Sponsor') and second, Hensthorpe Athletic Association Football Club (founded 1926) (hereafter referred to as 'the Sponsorship Vehicle'). The agreement being subject to approval by the Boards of Directors of both institutions, and the final approval of the Chairman of the Board of the Sponsor, J. O. Openshaw Esq.

Article 1: the Sponsor will establish a fund for the purchase of players and other key staff and the payment of their salaries and emoluments while under contract with the Sponsorship Vehicle. All expenditure subject to approval by the Managing Board of the Sponsor and the casting vote of the Chairman. Object: the acquisition of a first team of sufficient quality to enable the Sponsorship Vehicle to progress rapidly into the higher levels of the Nationwide League and beyond.

Article 2: the Sponsor will establish a development fund for the creation of a youth team and the inception of suitable community development projects of potential benefit to the Sponsorship Vehicle. Approval of all expenditure subject to Article 1 arrangements. Object: the establishment of the long-term future of the Sponsorship Vehicle, improving its standing in the community locally and nationally, etc.

Article 3: the Sponsor will commission a study into the development and realisation of a new sports complex facility, including new all-seater stadium, training facilities, and a leisure complex. Object: creation of suitable facilities for the maintenance of the Sponsorship Vehicle as a leading association football club within the structure of the English Football Leagues.

Article 4: the Sponsorship Vehicle will promote the image of the Sponsor at all times, in particular through the use of suitable promotional and advertising material and through community and other events. Object: to create a strong image for the Sponsor and the Sponsorship Vehicle.

Article 5: the name of the Sponsorship Vehicle to be 'Gary United Association Football Club', or commonly 'Gary United'...

At this point, Jack flung down his pen in disgust. 'I'm sorry, Murray, I just can't agree with this. I mean, what do we want a wally name like this for? It's just a joke. Doesn't make no sense at all.'

Murray laid his hand on Jack's arm. 'But it does make sense, Jack, don't you see. You're right - of course it's a joke - just the sort of catchy, trendy joke that'll appeal right away to the football-loving masses, and the media. Just like the silly names some of these pop groups give themselves - you'll see, it'll not just be a name, it'll become a totem. And to support it fully that way - this is the one bit I haven't fully told you about yet - the club will have a founding commitment only to give contracts to footballers with the name Gary.'

'You what? Murray, have you gone completely bonkers? I mean, the basic idea, yes, I buy that all right, but... this is just madness, just complete, utter madness, this is...'

Murray nodded his head, slowly. 'Yes, Jack... madness is just exactly what it is - what it's intended to be. And it's because it's madness, because it'll come across as a joke, that it'll succeed, so that ultimately the sky's the limit as to what the thing might achieve.'

He pondered for a moment, drumming his fingers on the boardroom table.

'You see... has it ever occurred to you, Jack, how many really good, really talented professional footballers are called 'Gary'? I don't know why it is - it just is, and that's the fact.'

*****

Footballers called Gary? It was preposterous, of course it had never occurred to him. He knew about Gary Lineker, of course, and maybe there were one or two others he'd come across, but mostly they were retired now, and then, of course - there was young Gary Hopkiss who played for the lads on the left wing, was one of the best players, in fact, if only he had a bit more opportunity to do his stuff...

'You're barmy, Murray, that's what you are. OK, I agree with you, it's catchy, an' all that stuff. But it's just not realistic. I mean, even if these characters exist, if they're any good they're not going to want to know, are they? I mean, 'Hensthorpe Athletic', it's not exactly Liverpool, or Chelsea, or even Bolton bloody Wanderers, is it...'

'No, Jack, that it isn't. But we can build things up gradually. I'm not talking about making a move for any of the top players, not initially at any rate, but there's lots and lots of good, solid professional Garys kicking around the Nationwide League, or with some of the lower-profile Premiership clubs. Not world-beaters, but the sort of players who can hold a team together, get results, get promoted. I've already identified quite a few. So, we get hold of some of these players. Then we make steady progress through the intermediate leagues, till we're on the threshold of Premiership status. Then we go after the big names, the superstars, the players who can make a thing of Gary United on the European and world stage.'

'Completely barmy, Murray, completely barmy. I mean... even these 'solid professionals' you're talking about, even if we paid them enough, I mean, the Unibond League Division Two, that says it all, don't it...?'

'But we can swing that one, Jack. Like I said earlier, I've done my research, and you wouldn't believe how cash-strapped all these lower leagues are these days. Even the Nationwide League... well, I've had quite a few informal discussions, and it's like this: if we guarantee to improve the club facilities, and put in place a team that no-one can deny would be out of place at a higher level, and we buy out of the Unibond and the Vauxhall Conference with a one-off payment, and then we guarantee the Nationwide League a certain sum per year over the first five years of the club's membership - and I'm talking about quite reasonable sums of money for all of this - well, I've been assured we could be given a place in the Third Division for our first season, at the very least...'

Jack was rapidly becoming nonplussed. He still couldn't believe any of this was going to work, but he couldn't just out with it and say so because, he knew Murray would have the answer to all his objections, just like he always did. He knew, as well, it was going to be very, very expensive, but he didn't mind spending the money as long as it was an investment, money well spent, and here again he knew that with Murray it would be, it always was. As usual, he was being cornered into picking up his faith in both hands like some bloody great, priceless Ming vase or something, leaving everything up to Murray as per usual, though as per usual he wasn't going to cave in completely without putting up some kind of a fight.

'OK, OK, Mr Clever Clogs, I expect you're right as per usual. So let's get things a bit more... specific, shall we? You seem to know all this stuff - so which of all these bloody millions of players called Gary have you decided to go for, to start out with, to get the ball rolling so to speak, if it's not a rude question or what...'

'Yes, Jack, I've got a few players in mind, in fact with some of them I've already been talking to their agents about transfer fees and so forth - no, don't worry, strictly on an informal basis, you understand. Well, let me see, there's

Gary Harkness who's looking for a transfer away from Everton as I understand, and Gary Entwhistle, the young Crystal Palace forward, and Garry Gayle of Huddersfield, he's a good, solid central defender...'

Jack's feeble pretence of stubbornness, of kicking against the pricks, trickled out of his brain like warm, sticky jelly. Tentatively, he grasped hold of the Ming vase and weighed it in his hands.

'I don't like the sound of this, Murray, I don't like it at all... I mean, whatever you say about it, it's still just complete madness at bottom, I mean isn't it...'

Slowly, deliberately, Jack picked up again his ballpoint pen, and at Murray's bidding continued in his role as reluctant scribe. Article 5 of the constitution of Gary United finally read like this:

Article 5: the name of the Sponsorship Vehicle to be 'Gary United Association Football Club', or commonly 'Gary United'.

*****

2. Creating the dream: 2002 - 2007

Dom Pegley, Chief Sports Reporter for the Hensthorpe and Bogham Argus (February 2007): 'It may have been sheer pity for the Grimsby Town players that caused Sam James, the match referee, to blow the final whistle a full five minutes before the 90 was up, by my reckoning. No sooner had he done so than the majority of these players sank, as if exhausted, to the pitch. And exhausted they surely were -

mentally more than physically - having succumbed on their home ground to the biggest drubbing ever inflicted on a team in the history of the football league in England.'

Seventeen - nil had been the final score. Almost all the outfield players had bagged at least one goal, and Gary Hopkiss, the flying winger now being talked of as a probable for the England squad, made a double hat-trick. It had been phenomenal - even the growing army of travelling fans ('the Ghastly Garys') were struck dumb at the end, hardly able to believe what they had seen.

'D'you think we'll make the playoffs, this time, then?' Jack whispered hoarsely to Murray Alexander-Walker, in the Grimsby Directors' Lounge after the game.

He sipped gingerly at his gin and tonic. It was sickening - automatic promotion to the Premiership would have been a foregone conclusion, had it not been for the 15 points per season penalty the Nationwide League had imposed on the club as part of the price of special admission, three seasons ago; a penalty that had not stopped them, in successive seasons, from progressing almost without difficulty from the third division, then from the second, until now they stood on the verge of the Premiership itself.

Murray's reply was unhesitating. 'Surely we will, Jack, surely we will. A win like this - it creates its own momentum, you'll see if it doesn't. Did you see the state of the lads after the game, in the dressing room? They're so fired up, they've got the opposition so scared, they've practically won the rest of this season's games already, without even kicking another football.'

Indeed, the dressing room high jinks Jack had briefly witnessed - before fleeing shamefacedly to the sobriety of the Directors' Suite - had been almost as unbelievable as the game itself. Gary Hopkiss had been force-fed shampoo and Guinness until he vomited all over the floor. A dazed Grimsby Town player found wandering distractedly in the corridor had been manhandled into the dressing room and was being forced to perform various vaguely obscene acts with the Garys goalkeeper.

'You gave him fuck all to do during the game, mate, so you'd better do something to perk him up a little now...'

One of the Grimsby directors, yellow-faced and drawn, bravely wandered over to offer his congratulations.

'I'd never have believed it... it's not humiliating, not really, because it's just a one-off. Our players, they're not bad players at all, but what you've got going with this new set-up of yours, it's phenomenal, just phenomenal...'

Yes, Jack reflected, it really was phenomenal, he'd never have believed it could have gone like this, two and a half years ago. Now, he was so used to the euphoria, even a win like this didn't seem that special, it was just another small step up the now-conquerable Everest of his and Murray's ambition. An Everest whose absolute summit was still invisible, but they'd climbed so high now he'd got used to the altitude, he didn't feel dizzy and breathless anymore when he looked upwards.

The Grimsby director wandered away; Murray, however, was still at his shoulder. 'Of course, we mustn't take things for granted, Jack. A great win, I agree, but we're still not ready to take on the European League big boys, and stuff them good and proper, too. We've got to build further towards next season - our first in the Premiership. Now..." he paused, and licked his lips with the tip of his very pink tongue, "there's this Ukrainian player I've been having a look at, big central defender, name of Sergei Garishnikov. He's a great player, he'd go down well with the media and the fans with his name and face and all, I understand his agent's looking for around 15 million - dollars, that is, not pounds...'

Jack nodded, swallowed his gin and tonic, and thought weakly about the ways of life.

*****

It hadn't been at all easy, not at first. Not because of all the money, the colossal layout on the stadium, the advertising, the new players. Not in handling all the complicated negotiations, with property developers, football league officials and the like. Jack had inwardly anticipated problems there, and of course, just as always, they had not materialised, but other problems had popped up in other, unexpected areas.

The first little difficulty had occurred with the sacking of Colin Allardyce, the original team coach. Jack had never liked Allardyce much, and knew in his heart of hearts he was lazy and incompetent. Despite the string of poor results, Allardyce hadn't expected to see his meal ticket taken away without notice, and although he expressed little surprise when Jack called him in to give him the bad news, he went straight away to the local newspaper with his story. He also threatened to take the club to an industrial tribunal.

None of this, in itself, posed much of a threat. Allardyce had been handsomely paid off for the cancellation of his contract, and he hadn't made many friends in the locality in the two years since he took charge of the team. But a newspaper reporter on the local daily started sniffing around, and twigged that something was up, and started spreading rumours that something big was happening, before Jack and Murray were really ready to make the details of their plans public.

*****

Dom Pegley, Chief Sports Reporter for the Hensthorpe and Bogham Argus (February 2003): 'It has come to our notice, from a confidential (but highly reliable) source, that something highly disturbing is afoot with 'the Hensmen'. Despite the recent run of poor results in the League, the owners appear to be bent on condemning the old club to its complete destruction. Currently managerless, rumour has it that the principal asset, the Nailmaker's Row ground itself, is to be sold off with all profits going straight into the directors' pockets. We are also given to understand that plans are afoot to relocate this famous old club 30 miles south to Congleton, Cheshire and to rename the club 'the JC Congers'. Leaving Hensthorpe and Bogham with no proper football team closer than the hated Stockport County, our deadly rivals, and dealing a massive blow to the spirit of the community.'

Stockport County would indeed probably have been

Hensthorpe's deadly rivals, except that the two teams had never met competitively – Stockport always being at least four divisions higher than 'the Hensmen' in the football pyramid – so Pegley's article was, in this as in other respects, largely incorrect. Nevertheless, the appearance of it caused quite a stir in the local community. Jack and Murray knew they would have to do something about it, and quickly. Knowing Pegley quite well, Jack called him and invited him to come over so he and Murray could set things straight.

The discussion again took place in the Garrymore Holdings boardroom. Jack left it entirely to the boy Murray to open the dance.

'We won't ask you to name your source,' Murray began, 'although as you might expect, we've a pretty good idea of who it is. We're not saying, either, that what you wrote in your article is *entirely* wrong: although it is in many ways, and certainly in those ways that are, shall we say… detrimental to the standing and aspirations of the football club.'

'Oh yeah? I'm waiting to hear you putting me straight, then.' Pegley eyed Murray suspiciously; he was a smallish man with sharp black eyes and very bushy eyebrows, who looked rather like a character from 'Lord of the Rings' – a wizard perhaps, or a suspicious, unfriendly dwarf. He had rather a high opinion of himself and didn't much care (as Murray knew well) if what he wrote was inaccurate, as long as it had maximum effect in boosting the newspaper's rather modest circulation.

'Of course we will, Dom, of course we will. We know the influence your articles have in the local community, and we both respect your judgement and integrity. The first thing, now, well, it is true we are planning to relocate the club to a new stadium.'

'A new stadium in the vicinity of Congleton, Cheshire, perhaps?'

'Not at all, Dom, not at all. Look here, Jack and the directors have very ambitious plans for the club, certainly beyond anything you might imagine. But all of this will take place exclusively within the orbit of the community – of Hensthorpe and the immediate surroundings – we can assure you of that.'

Pegley continued to eye Murray and Jack suspiciously. He regarded both of them as unscrupulous entrepreneurs who couldn't be trusted in the least. This was wholly unfounded, but stemmed from Pegley's inherent bitterness following a long career in journalism that had somehow never taken off in the way he felt his talents merited.

'Assurances are one thing,' he grumbled, 'but the facts of the matter are what concern me and the facts I've been given don't at all square up with what you're telling me now.'

He threw himself back in the big boardroom chair (he'd been given the place of honour at the table in deference to his investigative reporting skills) and continued to glare beadily at his interlocutors.

'Well, Dom, it's like this,' continued Murray soothingly, 'We have our plans – big plans – and we can tell you something about them, but at this moment in time a lot of our thinking must remain confidential. You'll see, very soon indeed, how we intend to take things forward. But it can't happen all at once, and a good deal of it is rather sensitive.'

Pegley opened his mouth to say something sarcastic, but Murray carried on with a wave of his hand.

'It's all about timing, you see. There are some aspects of our plan that we can tell you about now and that we're happy for you to publish – indeed that would be helpful to us if you *did* publish them – and then there are some aspects we can tell you about, but that you must keep confidential until we give you the go-ahead, not too far away I can assure you. And then there are some aspects that we just can't tell you about at this moment in time; but I can promise you, they are very exciting and absolutely in the best interests of the club and the local community.'

Murray paused, thus allowing Pegley this time to pour his sarcasm onto the *tapis*.

'This is all very fine – very fine indeed – but no different from the sort of stuff I've heard millions of times before. That's one of the secrets of successful investigative journalism, you know, sorting the fact from the fiction, and what you're telling me comes over as a good deal more fiction than fact. I know my sources, and I just can't believe what you're spinning me, Murray, I can't believe it at all.'

Murray laid his hand on Dom Pegley's arm. 'Listen, Dom,' he said, 'you know I trust your integrity and your professionalism. What I'm about to tell you concerns the new stadium, the development of the team as a proper professional outfit, and quite a bit of other stuff as well. We promise to give you exclusive access to all aspects of our planning, as long as you agree with our requirement to hold back for the time being on certain items of information. Purely in the interests of the club, you understand, but we *guarantee* you will be the first to know of all future developments, which I'm sure will prove to be very exciting to your subscribers and eventually to a much, much wider audience – a global audience, in fact. Agreed? OK, well in that case, let me tell you what we have in mind about the stadium, which is something we'd be more than happy for you to publish in the Argus at the earliest opportunity...'

And Murray told him. Despite Dom Pegley's limitations as a reporter, both he and Jack largely trusted him when pointed in the right direction, and tantalising promises of more exclusives about Hensthorpe Athletic were virtually guaranteed to keep him loyal to the cause. The meeting ended with handshakes all round, Jack once again marvelling at Murray's unerring ability to pull the irons from the fire. That was why he himself had kept so uncharacteristically quiet the whole time.

Dom Pegley, Chief Sports Reporter for the Hensthorpe and Bogham Argus (March 2003): 'Following our exclusive report concerning 'the Athletic' a week ago, it has been brought to our attention that certain facts we were assured were fully correct, are in reality a distortion of the truth. In point of fact, some exciting developments are afoot concerning our famous old club. I now have it *on good authority* that there will indeed be a move to a new stadium, to be developed on a brownfield site (probably the site of the old fireworks factory) just a stone's throw outside the Hensthorpe town limits. The plans include an all-seater ground with space for 30,000 spectators, hospitality suites, under-pitch heating, all mod cons in fact. And alongside this, significant improvement of the playing squad with a view to full professional status and advancement up the leagues over the next five years....'

*****

A second little difficulty arose a few years later, with the appointment of a new manager. By this time, the club (still called Hensthorpe Athletic) had made good progress on its journey upwards and was on the cusp of promotion to the Nationwide Championship (or 'the old bloody Second Division' as Jack derisively called it).

Initially, following the dismissal of Allardyce, Jack and Murray had decided to appoint a safe pair of hands – someone with solid lower-league experience as player and manager - a bit of a feel for the football environment in the Northwest of England, and a determined but undemonstrative personality. Thus it was that they paid Crewe Alexandra the grand sum of £200,000 to obtain the release of their highly respected manager, Stuart White, to come in on a three-year contract.

White soon proved himself to be the ideal man for the job. He had the contacts to bring in some decent players to improve the team to Football League level, he managed things without fuss and got the team playing cohesively and well. Above all, he understood and bought into Jack's ambition. As a result, by the time the three-year contract reached its term, and following the rather expensive and very controversial purchase of a place in the Nationwide League (League Two – the old bloody Fourth Division), 'the Latics' had progressed to the Championship two levels higher; had settled into their new home, the Garrymore Arena (named after the club's main sponsor); and looked a dead cert for further progress to the heady snowfields of the Premier League. The sense of excitement in the town and its surroundings, and the sense of amazement in the football community as a whole, were – as the expression goes – almost palpable.

At this time, the club had still not attempted to change its name to 'Gary United'. The necessary papers were prepared, a number but not all of the recently recruited playing staff were indeed called Gary, but most senior players still were not. Both Jack and Murray understood what a stir would be caused by the transition, and though prepared for it, Jack was still fundamentally very uneasy about what he saw as simply a too-clever bit of commercialism.

'I still don't like it, Murray lad, just don't see the point of it. Oh, don't get me wrong, what we've managed to do so far – what *you've* managed to do, in fact – is nothing short of a bloody miracle. Never really believed it could actually happen. But I just don't want us to bugger things up, that's all. We'll be in the Championship next season, you know – probably. What's it going to look like, I mean, 'Gary United' alongside teams like Sunderland, an' West Brom, an' Blackburn Rovers an' all....'

'Don't worry about it, Jack, just don't worry. Trust me. I

know it seems preposterous, in a sense it actually is preposterous, but football's changing, you know. There really is a global audience now, and if we're going to get interest in places like Bangkok and Baltimore, we need something different, something catchy, to draw the public away from the Manchester Uniteds and Chelseas of this world. You'll see. It really is the *absolutely necessary* final step we need to take to catapult the club into the international arena...'

Jack grumbled a bit more, and adopted the same hangdog expression he often resorted to when clinching his business deals, but he knew he was no match for Murray in an argument of this sort.

'Another thing, Jack. Stuart's managerial contract comes to an end at the end of this season. He's a good man, he's done wonders for the club, but I don't see him operating as well at Championship level and above. We'll have to replace him with someone a little more – high profile, someone with European experience – probably a foreign manager, in fact. No, don't look so miserable about it; we can offer Stuart a very good backroom role if he wants it, or a handsome payoff if he doesn't. I've kind of been sounding him out about it a little, he's a decent man and he has the interests of the club at heart.'

Jack grunted; he was far from happy. And in fact, up to point he was right: the new manager would be Murray's first and only real mistake in the ascent of the footballing Everest.

*****

The new manager Murray had in mind was an Italian, rather neatly called Garibaldi Guidonelli. His CV included spells with several clubs in the Italian First and Second Divisions, impressively including a good run to the semi-finals of the UEFA Cup a couple of seasons before with an Italian team that had rather ungenerously been described by the sports media as 'performing beyond expectations'.

'What the hell do we want a bloody Wop manager for?' Jack had churlishly replied, when Murray told him. 'He'll probably take the team backwards – look at all those bloody Italians running backwards in the Second World War, don't s'pose he'll be any different.' World War II mythology figured quite prominently in Jack's historical psyche.

'Not at all, Jack, not at all. He's just what we need at this period in our development,' Murray insisted. 'Not one of the really big names, but a good record of taking emerging teams further up the ladder - if we can agree on terms, we offer him a two-year contract, you see.'

'Don't bloody well see at all. Oh, I get it, with the name 'Garibaldi' and what have you. But I don't s'pose I'll be able to trust him farther than I can throw him. Stuart's doing a good job. Don't see it at all.'

In truth, Murray was perhaps somewhat beguiled by the 'Garibaldi' moniker. The club had finally taken the big step of renaming itself 'Gary United', to the amazement and glee of the footballing press and the world of football in general, and this would be the cherry on the commercial cake as far as he was concerned.

Garibaldi's job interview with the directors was an interesting affair. He was not at all what the directors were expecting; instead of a stereotypically excitable, butterfly-like, opera bouffe Italian with comically broken English, they were confronted with a rather heavy, serious-faced man with very fixed ideas and a command of English that was, if anything, rather too perfect.

Things didn't start off too well. The four directors (Jack and Murray included) were rather wary and uncertain of how to deal with a foreigner, while Garibaldi simply sat in his chair across the table, eyeing them stolidly. After a few initial pleasantries, the ball was opened by Mike Stotfold, a recent appointment to the board and golfing crony of Jack's.

'So, Mr er… Goodoldjelly,' he began, speaking loudly and distinctly as one always should to a bloody foreigner, 'if – we – appoint – you – as – manager, can - you - please - explain – how - you - would – propose – to – take – the team – forward – now weareheadingfortheChampionship.' The last few words coming out all in a rush, Stotfold (a rather fat man) being rather exhausted by his prior efforts at clear articulation. 'DO YOU UNDERSTAND WHAT I AM SAYING?' he shoutingly concluded, having got his breath back and wanting to ensure Guidonelli took in at least part of the question.

Guidonelli sighed and shrugged his shoulders. 'Of course, of course.' he replied, wearily. 'Although, as you know, I have no previous experience in English football, I am convinced my methods can be transferred successfully to the Championship sphere. You will have studied my methods, of course; they are built on solid training, a strong work ethic and above all, dedication to the collectivity of the team. I may say that teamwork, more than anything else, is the key to successful results in football.'

'BUT HOW CAN WE BE SURE OF THAT? WE NEED TO BE SURE!' Stotfold roared across the table. Being unused to interviewing and therefore rather nervous, he had simply not noticed that Guidonelli's command of English was rather better than his own, and having once got up to the cadence of shouting he simply let fly the first words that came into his head.

'Well, as I was just saying, you need to look at my methods and my results – with Sporting Club Capuccino and Atletico Affogato in particular. Of course, in making any managerial appointment there must be a degree of taking things on faith – taking a risk, if you like. But I feel sure that in my case the risk really is minimal – very minimal indeed.'

Stotfold spluttered incoherently, he really was nonplussed and was beginning to realise he was making a fool of himself. Fortunately, Murray, who hitherto had wanted the other directors to have their say whatever the outcome, came to his rescue.

'Of course, Mr Guidonelli, we understand there is always a risk. I think what Mr Stotfold wants is a bit more understanding of how you would apply your methods to our specific situation – as you know we are on a strong upwards trajectory, and need to be sure that with you this would continue.'

Guidonelli needed the job, being at the time out of work and having left his two previous managerial posts on rather less than amicable terms with his employers – a fact that, fortunately for him, was not widely known outside Italy. So he played expansively on what he could do for Gary United – how he could inspire the players to new levels of performance, how he had the contacts to bring in talented new recruits, how he could deal with inflated egos, how he intended to launch the club into the higher echelons of the Premier League, etc.; all the stuff, in fact, that the directors wanted to hear. He was so persuasive that the deal was concluded more or less straight away – with Murray's persistence it had been pretty much a foregone conclusion anyway. Even Jack was satisfied, although he didn't want to show it.

'Well, I s'pose he'll have to do. The lad seems to have some bright ideas, if he's not a bit too sure o' hisself. Don't seem much like an Italian at all. More like a bloody Londoner. You know – a bit cocky like, bit too sure of hisself, but maybe that'll do for now anyway.'

But in fact, on this occasion, Jack's original instinct proved to be correct. Guidonelli brought in a couple of Italian players who didn't fit in very well, and proved to be such a martinet on the training ground and on the touchline that he alienated most of the original players. Soon he was on bad terms with the directors, too. During the first season in the Championship, Gary United failed to meet the high expectations everyone had of them, languishing doggedly mid-table and even flirting briefly with relegation back to League One at one point. Guidonelli had to go. Following a brief interlude with Stuart White back in a caretaker role, he was replaced by another foreigner – a German, this time – name of Wolfgang Groschenpinscher. Wolfgang, despite his Teutonic name and origin, proved to be the absolute antithesis of the dour Italian: excitable, butterfly-like, opera bouffe etc., but he succeeded in righting the ship, getting Gary United back to winning ways the following season and on course for the Premier League. He was adored by the Ghastly Garys, and if something of a figure of fun in the sporting pages of the national press, sometimes mocked for his poor command of English, he was after all a successful one. Jack was beside himself, the day promotion to the Premier League was confirmed.

'Bloody marvellous,' he proclaimed, 'Bloomin' bloody marvellous. Never really dreamt it would happen. But now it has. We'll be takin' on Manchester United next season. They may be the champions, but now they've got us to reckon with, them without Sheringham an' Solskjær, an' all…'

3. Living the Dream: 2007 to 2013

'Please, Daddy, will you take us to the match on Saturday, I know we're going to win, oh, please, Daddy, please, please, *please...*'

Nine-year old Emily was hopping around on one leg in her stockinged feet, a look of excruciating, anticipatory anxiety on her freckled, snub-nosed face. Her older brother, Patrick, aged 11, being of a more stoical disposition, hovered behind her in the doorway to the living room, silent but hopeful.

'Well, I don't know… I'm working on Saturday morning,

you know… but maybe I could get back in time, if the kick-off's at three…'

'Oh, please, please, *please,* Daddy, I *know* you can get back in time…'

'Well, OK then, I'll see what I can do. If I can book the tickets, an' all…'

Gary United operated a 'family entry' scheme with special tickets available for adults bringing two or more children to the Garrymore Stadium on matchdays. Furthermore, it meant seats at the front of the grandstand, right next to the pitch, almost within touching distance of the players, many of whom were regarded by Patrick and Emily almost as living gods.

Despite his apparent reluctance, Barry Parkminder was secretly rather pleased at this opportunity to cheer on 'the Hensmen' - Gary United having retained this nickname in homage to their humble origins – so he went ahead and booked the tickets. They were playing Manchester United this particular Saturday afternoon – a big match. Barry knew his boss would let him leave a bit early on Saturday so he could make it back in time.

******

Barry Parkminder was an unremarkable man. He lived in an unremarkable semi-detached house in an unremarkable part of Hensthorpe, and worked unremarkably as the deputy manager of a building society branch in the centre of Manchester. Every workday he commuted from home and back by train to Manchester Piccadilly station.

Barry was very typical of the kind of man (or woman) who supported Gary United. That is to say, not someone who had a tribal association with the club – he wasn't even originally from Hensthorpe, in fact – but someone who had adopted it, and become proud of it, as it made its meteoric rise over a very few years from semi-professional obscurity into the Premier League. Like so many others, he was mesmerised by this rise, not just because it was so sudden and unprecedented, but because, in a way, it had happened against the tide of change in English professional football. By 2011, despite Roman Abramovitch, Stan Kroenke et al., it was becoming clear that the era of the billionaire private owner, for clubs at the very highest level least, was becoming more and more difficult. Manchester City had, three years before, been bought by the Abu Dhabi United Group and had immediately splashed out colossal sums on Robinho, Carlos Tevez, Emmanuel Adebayor and many more, the sort of ongoing outlay that even Jack Openshaw could only wince at. Furthermore, there simply weren't enough top-level Garys to compete any more with the influx of international superstars coming into the biggest clubs of the Premier League.

Still, for the time being, Gary United was holding its own, being mid-table in the Premier League with just a few games to go of the 2010-11 season.

Barry's wife, Christine professed to understand little about football.

'I don't know what you go to these games for,' she declared, on hearing about the Manchester United match, 'just to watch all those little men running about on the grass after a stupid football. And look at the sums of money they're paid! Would be better if some of that money went into the pockets of nurses, or teachers, or folks who actually do some real good in society.'

She sniffed, and put on the stony-eyed, vacant expression she always adopted when saying something she considered challenging; in fact Barry was used to it, as she had made this same declaration many times before. She was a part-time teacher herself, so she had quite strong feelings on the subject of the inflated salaries of professional footballers.

He sighed, understandingly. 'I know, I know, it doesn't seem right, does it, but that's life, I s'pose,' he replied, 'but just think! What a treat for Patrick and Emily! It's Manchester United – the greatest football club in history! Premier League Champions! Ryan Giggs! Wayne Rooney! Mame Biram Diouf!' Barry could get uncharacteristically carried away when talking about football, and Biram Diouf was, for some reason, a particular favourite of his.

'Huh! It still seems just stupid to me. Don't know what you, or anyone else, sees in it.'

Christine sniffed coldly again, determined not to be done out of her grievance. Secretly she was rather pleased that Barry was taking the children to the big game, seeing that it brought about bonding between them that few other of their family activities could achieve.

Although Barry was an unremarkable man, he was not an unthinking man. He was as aware as Christine of the need for bonding with his children, and – besides always enjoying watching a good game of football - was grateful to Gary United for giving him the opportunity to do so.

******

'Ooh, Daddy, why wasn't that a penalty? That *should* have been a penalty!'

The match had been underway for nearly 30 minutes. So far, not a great spectacle, a cagey beginning from both teams. Manchester United, already well clear at the top of the league table and not wanting to take any risks, had snuffed out the Garys' attacking threat. Gary Colhoun, the big, bustling centre-forward, seemed seriously out of sorts. Then Gary Hopkiss, the now-ageing but still swift and skilful winger who, until a couple of years before had still been an England regular, was clumsily upended on the edge of the box by Chris Smalling. From where Barry, Patrick and Emily were sitting it *did indeed* look like a penalty, but in fact it wasn't.

It didn't matter. Gary Hopkiss picked himself up off the grass and curled a beautiful free kick into the top corner of the net, just evading Edwin van der Sar's grasping fingers. One-nil to the Hensmen! Patrick and Emily went wild.

'Hooray! Hooray! We're going to win the league! We're going to win the league!'

Emily was jumping up and down on her plastic seat, Barry hoped she didn't break it. Even the usually stolid Patrick was screaming and stamping his feet. Their seats were quite close to the Manchester United dugout, and Barry noticed that Sir Alex Ferguson, who was on his feet at the edge of the pitch, had a face like purple thunder; he hoped he wasn't going to come across and bawl them out. To his relief Sir Alex didn't, after a while he sat down again, looking as if he had accidentally swallowed his chewing gum or something.

*****

The match progressed, a more open game now that Man U needed to score. It looked as if the Hensmen would make it in the lead to half-time, but in the dying seconds a cross was swung in by Patrice Evra, and Wayne Rooney volleyed home. One-all! It completely spoiled the burgers and fizzy drinks Patrick and Emily consumed at half-time; Emily was sulking, rather.

'It's not fair!' she whined, almost in tears. 'Why do Manchester United *always* score a goal in extra-time... I bet they paid the referee to keep the game going just until they *did* score. It's just not fair!'

Barry did his best to calm her down. She was so upset by the myth of 'Fergie Time', he was worried she wouldn't be able to keep down the burger, fizzy drink and chips.

'Oh, don't worry,' she eventually declared fiercely, 'I *know* we're going to win anyway. They can't beat us, those nasty, cheating beasts! We're going to win – I *know* we are!'

And she stamped her little feet, to reassure herself. They returned to their seats for the second half.

******

The second half started very much as had the first: a cagey, cat-and-mouse affair with neither side wanting to take any risks. Then, about 15 minutes in, one of the little weaknesses of Gary United that had sometimes undone them before, imperilled the situation.

Wolfgang Groschenpinscher had been prowling the touchline, gesticulating and screaming instructions to his players in his broken English. In general, during games the players had learned to ignore his histrionics, and just get on with things; a basic problem was, with most of them being called Gary, and with the imperfect English and all, it wasn't always obvious exactly who he was shouting at or what he was trying to say. But sometimes it was impossible to ignore him; somebody got confused, misunderstanding between the players arose, and this created an opening for the opposition.

That is exactly what happened on this occasion. Gary, the right-back thought he was being instructed to go further up the pitch, whereas in fact Groschenpinscher meant for Gary, the big central defender to cover the attacking runs of Scholes from midfield. This left a gap for Ryan Giggs to run into, and his cross from Manchester United's left was again met by Wayne Rooney, who again thumped the ball into the back of the net. Absolute disaster! Two-one to Man U! Barry, Patrick, Emily and all the other Gary United fans in the stadium were stunned into a horrified silence. Groschenpinscher screamed and gesticulated even more loudly than before, but it made no difference. The Manchester players went efficiently about their business and sought to exploit the gaps developing in the Garys' defence as they stormed forward in search of an equaliser.

Groschenpinscher may have been something of a clown, but he was a shrewd, canny reader of the game of football. In the past, he had frequently managed somehow to turn around a sticky situation during an important game, and that was what he attempted to do now. With 15 minutes of the game left, he sent on the 19-year-old Brazilian striker Gary United had acquired on loan during the January transfer window, name of Anderson Riveleno dos Gravos Santos – or, as he had been dubbed by the Gary United fans, 'Garinyho'.

The introduction of Garinyho again changed the situation completely. He provided a new focus, not just for the attack, but as a distraction to the other players from the increasingly wild and incoherent comportment on the touchline of Groschenpinscher. This, allied to the fact that Garinyho really was an eager, fast and skilful attacking player, gave a new impetus to the previously ineffective Gary United forward play. Within five minutes of his introduction, he had dribbled his way into the Manchester penalty area to score an equaliser; then, deep into injury ('Fergie') time, he latched onto a pass and stroked the ball into the bottom corner of the net. The Parkminder family, and all the other Gary United fans in the Arena went wild, wild, wild! Hooray! Three-two, the final score!

It was their greatest victory of the season. Emily was jubilant, too excited even to vomit up her burger and fizzy drink. Holding her daddy's hand, she floated out of the Garrymore Arena on a wave of pure, unadulterated happiness, to be brought down to earth outside by the attentions of a news reporter, who in fact happened to be our old friend Dom Pegley, who gave her to understand he wished to interview her.

'So, little miss, what did you think of all *that?* You must be over the moon, I should think…'

'Yes, it was brilliant, just brilliant! I'm so excited I could scream! Of course, I *knew* we would do it in the end...'

'Oh really? How come you knew that?'

'Well, you see, I knew *anyway,* but then in the second half after they'd scored there was a throw-in just in front of us, and Wayne Rooney came over to take it. I could tell he was really cocky like, he *winked* at me like as if to say, 'that's it, you're finished now, you're not going to win'. So I *put a spell* on him, and that was it, I *knew* it would work and we *would* win in the end...'

It was quite surreal, they carried on home, jubilantly. Even the curmudgeonly Christine was happy and excited. She didn't really understand, of course, but knew that as far as her kids were concerned it had been a great, great day out, and that was enough for her.

******

Sir Alex was gracious in defeat. He accepted the offer of a drink from Jack in the Directors' Lounge after the game (he declined the G and T and opted for his habitual glass of claret) and complimented him and his team on their performance.

'Didn't think it was possible… once that second goal of ours went in, told myself that was it… don't know what to make of that clown of a manager of yours, though...'

He could afford to be charitable. Manchester United went on to win most of their remaining games that season, and topped the Premier League title by a full nine points over Chelsea and Manchester City. Gary United finished sixth.

For Jack – now well into his 70s, and still chairman of the club (although most of the business was now done on his behalf by Murray and others) – it was a crowning success, the first time in its history the club had actually beaten Manchester United. Beaten Manchester United! Like Emily, he could hardly believe it. For some reason his mind went back to the hotel room in Karachi all those years before, and his disappointment and frustration when Murray told him the result of that Champions League game….

******

A few days afterwards, Murray called him on his mobile.

'Got something to tell you, Jack. It's quite important. We've had an offer to buy the club, you see.'

Jack nearly choked on his drink (another G and T); he was relaxing at home, still luxuriating in the great success of the weekend before.

'To buy the club? Well, it's not for sale anyhow, no bloody way. Anyway, what's so special about that? We've had offers before, you know, don't see why you can't send this lot packing just like all the bloody rest...'

'I know, Jack, I know. But this time it's a bit different. It's the Qatari Government. Oh, not directly of course, they'd launder it through some so-called investment fund or what have you, but the sky's the limit in terms of price… it's a very good thing, as long as you're not put off by the ethical side of it, of course...'

But Jack *was* put off by the ethical side of it. The 2022 World Cup had been awarded to the Qataris by FIFA just the year before, in very murky circumstances. Jack hadn't liked it at all. He would never have called himself a football activist, but – just like Barry Parkminder, in fact – he was unhappy at the direction the highest levels of professional football were taking. It wasn't exactly to do with the colossal sums of money being thrown around, or globalisation, or even 'sportswashing' as such; but he was proud of what he and Murray had achieved, proud of the club in itself, and somehow, he sensed that any kind of a sell-out would in fact be just that: a sell-out. A sell-out of the magical rise of Gary United from its humble beginnings, of all the people who had made it happen and who in many cases were *still* making it happen. Despite the way football was going, he and Gary hadn't reached the end of their journey yet. So he gave Murray rather a sharp reply to his question, swallowed the rest of his drink and banged down his empty tumbler on the little japanned side table that always stood by the comfy chair in his living room, chipping off some of the lacquer.

'OK, Jack, I understand, of course. I had to ask you the question though, hadn't I? Actually, I'm very, very glad you don't want to sell. It would be a betrayal, that it would, and I wouldn't have wanted a part of it, even though the Qataris would surely have offered me a role on the board and a share of the ownership...'

In fact, Murray had guessed in advance what Jack's response would be. He had only really asked the question as a sort of test of faith, to make sure in his own mind that Jack's resolve concerning the grand scheme was as strong as ever.

******

4. Jack's Funeral: 2022 and in Retrospect

Jack died early in 2022, at the age of 85. He had stood down as Managing Director of Gary United some 10 years before, to be replaced on the board by his elder daughter, Justine. By then, he had had the satisfaction of seeing his beloved club safely established in the Premier League, then was able to watch from the sidelines as success built upon success. By 2022, Gary United had still not won the Premier League, but had finished in third place on two occasions, and had performed creditably in the European Champions League, defeating both Juventus and Barcelona in memorable games at the Garrymore Arena, and progressing once to the semi-finals. But some years earlier, Jack and Murray (who had taken over as MD) both knew that the dream was over. International football had a very different aspect to how it had been when G. United first reached the Premier League in 2007, let alone when the grand scheme began back in 2002. The era of the multi-billionaire club owner, as they had realised as long ago as at the time of that memorable defeat of Man U, was largely over, for the very top international clubs, at least. Gary United now had to compete financially with the likes of the Manchester Cities, the Arsenals, and on the international stage Real Madrid, PSG etc.; clubs backed by the almost limitless (and well-sportswashed) funds of oil-rich states and their agencies, and the like. The transfer fees and salaries paid to top professionals were almost beyond belief. No, it was no longer possible. The best they could hope for was continued presence in the top half of the Premier League, maybe some years competing in the Europa League or whatever new second-rate European club competition UEFA dreamed up next.

It was also the case that, by the mid-2010s, the forename 'Gary' was no longer as prevalent in the UK as it had been 10 or 20 years earlier. Due to the dwindling supply of available and sufficiently skilful Garys, the club had needed to compromise on its original policy in this respect, with no more than one or two 'token' Garys featuring in and around the first team squad from 2014 onwards.

Jack had loved his daughter dearly, and despite Justine having received what Jack derisively termed 'a bloody university education' she was in many ways as down-to-earth as her father. The funeral was a fairly modest affair. Jack had always declared he didn't want to be cremated, so he was buried discreetly in a modest plot in the churchyard of Hensthorpe Parish Church. There had been several hundred mourners at the service, however – Barry, Patrick and Emily Parkminder included - bearing witness to Jack's solid standing and popularity in the local community.

'Well, that's it then,' said Justine to Murray, as they walked away from the churchyard into the Hensthorpe February gloom. 'Just as he would've wanted it, I s'pose. He was a contented man, when all's said and done, a contented man.'

'D'you think so? There's unfinished business, you know: the Premiership title, the Champions League.'

Justine shook her head and laughed gently.

'I think he'd be contented enough with where we've got to. You know, the goalposts have moved rather a long way since he started out, almost literally.'

Murray said nothing for a while. They continued their slow walk along the path through the gravestones, to the rusty wrought-iron gate at the side of the church. Then he replied,

'That Gary Hopkiss, he's starting to make quite a name for himself with Burnley in the Championship. Very impressive for a first managerial post, y'know. I can see him coming to take over here in a few years' time; he'll be ready for it then, ready to step in and take on the big boys at their own game.'

'Yes – I'm sure he will – but we'll be the underdogs again by then, you know.'

'I know it, Justine, I know it – but does it really matter that much? We'll still be here, in the Premier League. Look at Blackburn Rovers. Founder members of the Football League back in the 1880s, and they're still in and around the top flight. How come a piddlin' little place like Blackburn can still mix it with the Arsenals and Liverpools and Real Madrids of this world?'

'Well, yes, I s'pose there's something in that...'

'And there's another thing, the boy Harkness, and one or two of the other Garys who've gone on in the game into management or whatever, they've spoken out about the way things are going: this World Cup in Qatar in particular. I mean, it's just an aberration, it's making a complete mockery of what we all stand for, of the beautiful game, an' all….'

Murray stopped mid-sentence in his reflections, becoming aware that by his side Justine Openshaw was indulging in a quiet chuckle.

'What's up, 'Tine? You don't agree with me? You don't think it's all a mockery? Come on, spit it out, lass...'

'No, Murray, it's not that I don't agree with you, in fact quite the contrary. But you know, for a moment I thought it was not you, but Jack talking. You sounded just like my dad...'

A Midsummer Night's Dream

I expect most people who know their Shakespeare would agree that 'A Midsummer Night's Dream' is one of his lightest, best and most enjoyable comedies. Attending a performance of it, in any circumstances, is surely guaranteed to put anyone into a happy, all's-right-with-the-world mood: a genuinely 'magical experience', diffused to the audience through the mystical scenario, the unfolding drama, the impossible mishaps, and the joie-de-vivre of the actors – whether amateur or professional. I suppose I've seen more than one performance of it, at the theatre or on screen, and have always come away thoroughly enlightened in spirit.

> *'Now, until the break of day,*
> *Through this house each fairy stray...*
> *And each several chamber bless,*
> *Through this palace, with sweet peace;*
> *Ever shall in safety rest,*
> *And the owner of it blest.'*

For me, the most memorable performance of the play I've ever witnessed was an outdoor performance given by an amateur theatrical society in the gardens of Gawsworth Hall, in Cheshire, in the summer of 1973.

****

I studied 'A Midsummer Night's Dream' as part of my G.C.E. 'A' Level course in English Literature at Abbeydale Grange Sixth Form College in Sheffield, between 1971 and 1973. This was the most difficult, tortured period of my adolescence, when I really didn't know what to do with myself at all, and although at the end of the course I came away with the top grade in my English Literature 'A' Level, the two years I spent at the Sixth Form College were, for various reasons, just about the most difficult of my whole life. Part of the problem was that I was desperately shy and insecure with girls, and the majority of the students taking the subjects I studied (English Literature, History and Maths) were female. I disguised my shyness under an unconvincing cloak of cynicism, cleverness and antisocial behaviour, which fortunately for me didn't wash at all when I went on to university, and which I therefore had to get rid of rather quickly.

The Gawsworth Hall performance took place in July, during the period after I'd taken all my 'A' level examinations but hadn't yet received the results. This was a period of relaxation for us students after all the weeks of hard studying and revising, not at all stressful because the exams were behind us, and we all knew there was nothing more to be done that could influence the outcome. It was our English teacher, Mrs Hunt, who found out about the planned performance of the play and suggested it as a coach trip to her class, as a treat and to keep up the spirit of camaraderie once the school year officially ended and we all went off in our different directions – to university, or the world of work, or wherever. The gesture was appreciated, and most of the students who had studied under her – between 20 and 30, I think – took up the offer.

It was to be an afternoon performance. We assembled at the sixth form college in the morning. It was a filthy day – heavy grey skies, wind and driving rain. Some questions were asked as to whether the performance could reasonably go ahead under such conditions, but we all climbed into the coach anyway and set off. From Sheffield, our route took us westwards into the Peak District, over the southern foothills of the Pennines to Ashbourne in Derbyshire and from there on to our destination. It rained all the way and was still raining when we arrived. I remember sitting next to John Harker on the coach. John was one of the very few other non-female students on the English Literature course, a heavy, rather dull-spirited boy who didn't do very well in the examinations. We tended to hang out together in the sixth form, playing bridge in the common room during the lunch breaks and sometimes going on illicit outings to the pubs in the vicinity of the college. We shared our packed-lunch sandwiches on the coach as we swished onwards through the rain - I remember wiping away the heavy, steamy film of condensation from the window with my sleeve as we passed through the outskirts of Uttoxeter, seeing the white-railed expanse of the racecourse lying mournful, sodden and poached under the rain as we drove by.

****

We arrived at Gawsworth. It was still raining, but not as hard as before, and the performance was scheduled to go ahead as planned. We all had raincoats and umbrellas, so we dispersed for an hour or so to wander round the grounds for a while before assembling for the spectacle. We took our places on the open stand overlooking the lawn where the performance was to take place – still wearing our waterproofs, but – wonder of wonders! the rain had gradually eased off, and now had ceased altogether. The sky was still heavy, grey and overcast, but it looked as if the gods had decreed in our favour after all. We settled down and waited for Theseus and Hippolyta to appear for Act I, Scene I.

There was a slight delay. Then one of the Company appeared from behind the canvas screen adjacent to the lawn. He had an announcement to make, which went something like this:

'Ladies and gentlemen – you'll be pleased to know that we're going ahead with the play as planned,' he explained. 'But unfortunately – because of the adverse weather we've had all morning, and the risk of further rain – we're not able to make use of the expensive costumes kindly lent to us by the Royal Shakespeare Company for the performance. We've done our best with the clothes and costumes we otherwise have available, but – please bear with us – it's a fairly motley assortment, no more than we could cobble together at very short notice. We request your understanding, we really mean to do our best to put on as good a show as we can, under the circumstances.'

The spokesman retired, and the play began. The spokesman was not wrong. The actors and actresses came on dressed in all kinds of unusual gear – odd, shapeless cloaks, funny floppy hats with feathers stuck in the brims, the most amazing, unfashionable stuff (unfashionable for the 1970s, that is) – anything they could find, I suppose, that resembled something akin to one's expectations concerning 16th-century couture in the context of the World of the Fairies and Athenian Woodland Sorcery. They did pretty well. They acted up, declaiming their lines in the clear air in strident, ringing voices, as actors generally do. One was enthralled by the spectacle, so that within five minutes of the performance starting one simply overlooked the fact that those involved were dressed in gear more appropriate to something between a Women's Institute *fete* and a down-and-outs' soup kitchen.

The performance continued up to the interval. The interval itself was enlivened by a carefully choreographed performance, delivered by a dozen or so of the little girls from a local primary school dressed as barefoot woodland fairies (probably, in this case, wearing the flimsy costumes as originally prepared for them by loving parents). They performed a routine involving synchronised diagonal runs across the lawn, with fairy crossovers in the middle, bearing aloft gauzy, pastel-coloured scarves that flowed back artistically from their outstretched arms as they ran. Their little feet splashed and sploshed across the sodden grass, raising the water to the surface in places in lambent, silvery pools. Brave little girls! They must have been chilled to the bone by the time their routine came to an end...

The rain still held off. The theatrical performance resumed after the interval, and... to oohs! and aahs! of amazement from the audience. The actors were continuing with Act IV arrayed in the gorgeous, sparkling finery supplied by the Royal Shakespeare Company. Titania, in a gorgeous green and gold robe and headdress, Oberon sneaking in behind, bottom all hairy and rustic, with his floppy ass's ears. And then – as much on cue as any of the entrances – but softly, discreetly, without any noticeable advance warning... the rain began to fall again.

What were they to do? Understandably, the actors on stage started to look distinctly uneasy. Should they retire in mid-scene and resume as before dressed in their glad rags? Should they abandon the performance altogether? One might speculate about what was going on behind the scenes….

Act IV, Scene I (bis): Close by a wood, Theseus and Hippolyta, looking distraught: enter a Stage Manager, even more distraught.

THESEUS:

> Once more the brawling wind doth wash the air,
> And we stand forth in finery display'd;
> Fair Hippolyta, think you once again
> In motley garments must we stand arrayed?

HIPPOLYTA:

> I fear the washing must perforce increase
> Its pace, bedaubing us; we must abandon all!

Something like that, anyway; in any event, the difficulty was solved by the stage manager, who scuttled out from behind the canvas with a number of umbrellas under her arm, each of which was unfurled and handed to the actors then performing. The show went on, the actors overcoming their initial sheepishness to perform bravely under their umbrellas, as the rain continued to fall right until the end of the performance… and at the end, they received a hugely appreciative ovation in recognition of their brave and resourceful effort!

****

I suppose that innovation - creating variety and freshness for an audience that has come to see a play that is not contemporary and is well-known to many of its members – is a major challenge for actors, producers, stage managers, all those involved in the performing arts. How do they respond to the challenge? In different ways - by their personal interpretation of plots and characters for example, by the sheer forcefulness of the on-stage performances, or by being 'modernistic', trying to create links with current political or social themes. I remember that in the 1970s there was a trend for performing Shakespearian drama in more recent (e.g., Victorian) costume, a rather unimaginative way to freshen up old perspectives and images. The Gawsworth Hall performance may not have been intended as anything more than a 'traditional' rendering of a well-loved work, but for me, even forty years later, it has left a lasting and still-vivid impression, all thanks to the English summer weather!

Trinidad Confidential

with apologies to Robert Smith Surtees

Part 1: The End of the Beginning (not the Beginning of the End?): February 2015

Even before the new Permanent Secretary started speaking, it was obvious that the project was finished, over, *terminé,* canned, kaput.

The new Permanent Secretary sat at the head of the table in the huge, windowless conference room, frowning slightly, her lips pursed, idly leafing through the dossier on the desk in front of her. On the front of the dossier was a small picture of a gaily-coloured hippo – the symbol of the consulting company that had undertaken the project; it was a copy of their inception report. The Permanent Secretary didn't look up, or speak, for some time, although she clearly wasn't studying the report very carefully. It was just a fairly obvious trick to rack up the tension, put the assembled consultants even more ill at ease than they must have been before they filed noiselessly into the room following her summons. And it was working - the consultants, six of them in all, now sat there still silent, holding their collective breath, trying hard not to fidget and become the particular subject of Permanent Secretarial attention. Any one of them looked as if he or she might, at any moment, utter a mad howl of anguish and flee headlong out into the reception area, to be free from this mental torture they were being so cruelly subjected to.

The Permanent Secretary was a cobra waiting to strike. For

the time being, she continued to hold the consultants in her sway, tantalising them completely into awestruck submission with her slightly raised eyebrows and contemptuous, mocking silence. She leisurely turned over a few more leaves of the inception report. The consultants were entirely spellbound, a timid and overawed huddle of mice, each of which quaked in the fear that he or she would be the first to feel the venom fangs puncturing his or her skin when the cobra finally decided on its move. But for now, the cobra continued to sit and read calmly, knowing that each silent second doing so just racked up the tension in the room even higher.

The Permanent Secretary may not have been a particularly clever person in an imaginative or forward-thinking sense, but she certainly knew how to keep her minions in thrall. At last, she looked up and spoke, drily,

"This report: it highlights many things that are not within our control. It doesn't really address the main issues facing us, does it? What do you have to say about that?"

There was an awkward silence for a few moments. Which of the consultants would be first to break cover? In the end it was Brendyn Bryman, the Project Manager, who bravely ventured a response,

"Well PS, our inception report was intended mostly to highlight some of the main problems facing the government as a whole, not just your ministry. Of course, we're aware that there are certain difficulties of communication between the MPA and the Public Service Commission, for example, and that these need to be addressed as a matter of urgency.

But as you'll see in the report, we've applied a quite sophisticated methodology in identifying the highest priority areas, based on stakeholder analysis and use of a weighted factor comparison system derived from the strategic objectives of the government's Gold Standard Modernisation Initiative…"

The Permanent Secretary cut short Brendyn's diversionary arabesques with a dismissive wave of her hand.

"But why highlight things we can do nothing about? Wouldn't it have been more appropriate to focus rather on those things that are <u>entirely</u> within the MPA's control? Doesn't it simply risk alienating the Commissioner General and other key figures by criticising their own efforts at reform in this way? After all, we have enough problems as it is gaining their support for our initiatives."

"No criticism of the PSC or anyone else is intended in our report, PS. But of course, we had to point out the most serious areas of difficulty, the ones that need to be addressed jointly by all the agencies concerned if the Modernisation Programme is to succeed…"

A faint but distinct snort of tired exasperation came from the Permanent Secretary.

"This is all very well in theory, but I just don't see how you expect me to proceed. What concrete steps are you actually proposing? What have you actually <u>done</u> in the six or seven months that you've been here? Carlton, can you shed any light on the subject?"

The Permanent Secretary turned to her deputy, a pensive-looking, middle-aged man sitting on her right.

"Well, PS, the consultants have correctly identified the main areas where work needs to be done. Of course, these were similarly specified in previous consultancy reports. I agree I would have expected more concrete progress by now, and while this may not entirely be the fault of Arnaque Consulting, it's disappointing they haven't shown a little more urgency or cohesion at times…"

Brendyn nodded vigorously, opened his mouth and launched into a further stream of phrases of smooth appeasement. He was a salesman at heart, so this sort of thing came naturally to him. It wasn't really working on this occasion, however; sitting at the other side of the table, his colleague Clovis Buckram closed his eyes and sighed. He for one wasn't fooled by the qualified nature of the Deputy Permanent Secretary's criticism; this, he knew, came from a man who was a confirmed enemy, a man known to have privately expressed to the PS his opinion that *'all the Arnaque consultants have been doing since they came to Trinidad is talk, eat and laugh amongst themselves in their project office'*. And despite his allegiances, Clovis had to admit that this wasn't a bad summary of how things had been on the project over the past six months.

It also struck Clovis that the conference room looked a lot like a funeral parlour; the dim lighting, the well-tended, glossy-leaved but sombre pot plants, the long, polished table leading away to the far end where reposed the tea and coffee-making paraphernalia and the large screen set into the wall for Skype conferences and PowerPoint presentations. If you replaced the screen with a set of curtains, you could place a coffin on the table and then trundle in down towards the curtains, then onward into an incinerator behind, just as in a crematorium… A coffin containing all the reports, all the presentations and workshop material, all the working documents and methodologies that Arnaque had inflicted on its client during those six months. Clovis shivered, not entirely as a result of the over-powerful air conditioning blasting its strong current of cold air into the conference room.

*

The Project Manager

By profession, Brendyn wasn't really a project manager. Sales and marketing was more his line. But he'd been an integral part of the selling of this project to the government of Trinidad and Tobago, and for one reason and another he had morphed from his original critical but non-managerial advisory role into the Project Lead. Initially quite excited at the prospect, he had very quickly found things a lot more difficult than he expected.

A Trini by birth, he had spent most of his working career in financial services in the City of London. Like a lot of people in financial services it was not altogether clear exactly what he had done, and he tended to be rather vague when questioned about the details of his *curriculum vitae.* Now, several career changes and two divorces later, he was back in the land of his birth, and coming rather to regret his decision to return.

He was a fine, off-hand, open-hearted, cheery sort of fellow, very easy to get on with and generally on excellent terms with his clients and colleagues (as well as with himself). The problem with Brendyn was, he was thoroughly, incorrigibly unreliable. If he arranged to meet you at a certain time on a certain date, the odds would be about ten to one on he would not show up. If he sent you an email asking you to be available for a Skype discussion at such-and-such a time, again, more likely than not you would be sitting at your computer screen waiting in vain for an hour or more for the anticipated 'ping' to come through. Brendyn also never seemed to put himself to the trouble of actually reading any of the reports or emails anyone sent him; with the result that he was generally pretty much in the dark about what was going on and what was being proposed to take things forward. His whereabouts were a mystery to his colleagues most of the time, it was generally supposed he was out and about in Port of Spain engaged in 'business development'; since his remuneration package with Arnaque Consulting was largely based on bonus payments for new work won rather than management of existing projects, this supposition was in fact largely correct.

The upshot was that Brendyn was almost the exact temperamental opposite to the standard mould of Project Manager, a species of control freak for which personal reliability was just one element in a strategy of keeping one's consulting team constantly under the collar.

Clovis, who over a long career as an independent consultant had worked under a good many of them, sometimes laconically remarked, "... *after all, they generally start out as quite decent people really, but they all turn vicious in the end"*. Brendyn was still quite decent, but definitely not in control (hence the talking, eating and laughing in the project office whether he was there or not) and up to now the viciousness was mostly confined to short, exasperated outbursts when he suddenly discovered there was something he ought to have done, but hadn't read the email telling him to do it.

"*Give him a couple more years,'* Clovis declaimed airily, *'give him a couple more years and he'll be just like all the rest – a snorting, green eyed beast"*.

The vagaries of the Arnaque Consulting's project for the Trinidad Ministry of Public Administration were such that it looked as if Clovis' prophecy would come true well ahead of time.

*

Part 2: Project Start-up: September/October 2014

Clovis was first alerted to the prospect of working in Trinidad by a phone call he received from his old friend, Damien Driscoll one fine summer's afternoon.

"Hello, Clovis, Damien from Arnaque Consulting here. I hope you are, ahh… keeping well. I know we haven't, ahh… been in contact for some time…"

When Damien spoke, he always sounded like a clergyman or a pompous solicitor – or maybe what he actually was, a partner at Arnaque Consulting. After a few more inconsequentialities about the weather and so forth, he came to the point,

"We have this, ahh… project coming up in Trinidad you may be interested in. We're preparing the proposal at the moment, and we, ahh… believe we have a very good chance of winning the work. We have a contact in Trinidad who is very close to the government, he has been helping to er… ahh… clear the way for us, and he will most probably act in some sort of, ahh… advisory capacity when we start to mobilise. We will, of course, put you in our proposal as a key expert with, ahh… many years of relevant experience and a high level of expertise…"

The 'contact in Trinidad' was, of course, Brendyn. After a few more minutes of verbal *escrime* concerning timescales, fee rates etc., some sort of agreement was reached and Clovis put the phone down. He didn't really expect to hear anything more about it, since only about one in ten of these project offers ever came off anyway, and the way this one was outlined to him sounded a bit odd in what it was expected to achieve. But then, a couple of months later, the phone rang again.

"Hello, Clovis. Damien again here. We, ahh… we won the project in Trinidad, and I was wondering when you would be available to start…"

Another cagey conversation followed concerning travel arrangements, expense allowances and other details. The work programme for the project still sounded a bit odd, but Clovis supposed this was because Damien was organising things to suit himself – being the soft, seriously overweight, plummy sort of person he was, he tended first of all to look after his own creature comforts rather than client requirements. Anyway, Clovis needed the work, and didn't want to jib unnecessarily at what was proposed – he knew that once Damien got a fixed idea into his head about something, it was as difficult to turn him as it was to stop a supertanker in its onward course - by the time you worked him round to a different approach, the problem the fixed idea was intended to address had dropped way astern anyway.

As it happened, by the time the project actually started in late September, Damien had resigned and left Arnaque Consulting. This gave his former colleagues at Arnaque ample opportunity to say exactly what they thought of him. In the early days, project conversational relaxation in the lobby bar of the Hyatt Hotel, Port of Spain after a hard day's consulting tended to gravitate towards Damien's many foibles, fallibles and failings.

"Of course, I wouldn't be on the project at all if he hadn't decided to go," declaimed Malcolm Shardlow. *"He never liked me very much, and that feeling was mutual. I always saw there was something not-quite-right about him. I heard that if he hadn't resigned of his own accord, he'd have been given the push anyway."*

Malcolm was a youngish, rather strait-laced project management specialist. Despite his normally rather old-fashioned demeanour, he did a very good impersonation of Damien, folding his hands across his stomach and looking glassily into the middle distance like some university professor declaiming,

"Well, yes, I, ahh… I think that would be a splendid thing to do… I, ahh… would certainly agree it would be quite splendid…"

Diane Willett, the project's M&E specialist, tried to demur. *"Well yes, I suppose he was something of a – I mean – a personality. I'm sorry. I mean, tell me if I'm repeating myself, but – I'm sorry – he <u>was</u> instrumental in putting this project together, as I understand it, so, - I'm sorry – we shouldn't forget that…"*

She stared around, looking uncomfortable and exposed; but then, Clovis thought, she *always* looked uncomfortable and exposed. She was always apologising, almost always when there was nothing to apologise about, she just seemed to have a nervous, irritating way of punctuating her conversation with 'I'm sorry's and 'forgive me if I'm repeating myself's. Evidently it was particularly irritating to Brendyn, who gave her an old-fashioned look back and growled slightly as he tucked into another spicy chicken wing. They were all sitting together at one of the tables in the lobby of the Hyatt Hotel in Port of Spain, an informal team meeting a week or so into the work programme to assess how things were going and (as Brendyn rather coarsely expressed it *'do a bit of bonking, er, sorry, I mean bonding'*).

"Oh, bullshit. Calling Damien a 'personality' is rather like calling a donkey a thoroughbred racehorse, in my opinion." The sneering riposte to Diane's feeble apologia came from Malcolm rather than Brendyn. *"There was something seriously wrong with him, you know. I heard there was some really unsavoury stuff, accessing pornographic websites, that kind of thing… I heard he was suspended for a while because of it a couple of years ago. 'Double D'! 'Donkey Damien'! Haw, haw, haw! That isn't a bad name for him,*

when I think of it!"

He guffawed and looked around, no doubt expecting some acknowledgement from his colleagues of his feeble witticism.

Brendyn, who was probably slightly drunk, was the only one who seemed to react. *"Donkey Damien! He's been divorced three times, don't you know? Obviously can't keep his pecker under control, just like a randy old donkey, in fact! Tee, hee, hee!"*

Clovis glanced idly around and yawned. Malcolm was such a bore; neither bonking nor bonding with any of his Arnaque colleagues struck him as a particularly interesting proposition at this moment in time. He felt weary, after a not-very-strenuous day at the office, pretending to read background material (mostly previous consultancy reports on the situation at the MPA) while actually most of the time playing Freecell on his laptop computer. Like most of the expatriate consultants on the project, he was staying at the Hyatt temporarily until more permanent accommodation could be found. Luxurious the Hyatt certainly was, but it was drearily antiseptic even by the dreary standards of five-star international hotels, like staying in a conference centre where everything was ultra-efficient, and everyone was ultra-attentive to the point of intrusion. He couldn't decide which would be less of a bore, staying on in the lobby to continue canoodling with the Arnaque project team, or go back up to his modernistic hotel room with its state-of-the-art bathroom fittings and huge plate glass window overlooking the harbour, and stare at the shipping.

In the end he opted to stay where he was. The spicy chicken wings and other perfectly presented *amuse-geules,* and the possibility of another free bottle of Carib Lager, swung it over the shipping. In the interests of personal amusement, he decided to be provocative.

"Anyway," he drawled, *"Damien may have been 'instrumental in putting the project together' as Diane puts it, but he seems to have left one or two convenient gaps in the terms of reference, hasn't he? What I mean is, here we are, more than a week into the programme, and it's not at all clear – to me at least – exactly what we are about."*

"What d'you mean? It's clear enough to me at any rate."

Brendyn glared at him savagely. Having been appointed Project Manager just a couple of weeks before, he tended to take any criticism personally. The mask of affability fell away. *'Project Managers: they all turn vicious in the end…'*

"Well," he continued, "I *refer to the Project Steering Committee Meeting just the other day. A steering committee is, presumably, intended to do just that – steer things along in the right direction – but most of the esteemed members just seemed to be half asleep, if anything."*

Brendyn laughed – rather nervously, it seemed, to Clovis. "*I agree they could have been a little more… dynamic,'* he said. *'But my feeling was that they were… well, sounding us out a bit. Yes, that's it, they were sounding us out – wanting to see what we have to offer, what our credentials are, that kind of thing.'*

'That's all very well; they're entitled enough to do that, I

s'pose. But even so, I was a bit disappointed. At the end I was just left wondering what we're actually here for. You know what I mean – are we advising, or doing? Doing or advising? No resolution on this from our somnolent friends on the committee. Of course, I know your views on the matter, but some sort of confirmation from the actual client would be quite helpful. It's all a bit 'queue de poisson', as the French would put it."

Clovis, who was very proud of his excellent command of French, was happy to trot out a phrase he knew Brendyn wouldn't understand. He professed to be an exponent of the 'doing' school of consultancy, and had been discomfited the previous day when Brendyn had ticked him off for wanting to get on with some actual work rather than read a few more reports.

"*You must understand, our role here is not to do project work for them,"* he had explained, *"but rather to give them guidance, make sure the projects they already have up and running are the right ones and are moving in the right direction. A light touch on the rudder, that's all – a light touch on the rudder."*

Clovis, who was getting tired of nautical metaphors and had in the meantime thankfully managed to extract his second Carib Lager out of the project budget, let the matter drop. He decided to take his change out of Malcolm instead.

"So – O' Project Management Specialist – I guess it's over to you then to take the lead in ensuring we advise properly, if that is actually what we're supposed to do. So - you were showing off your repertoire of materials the other day –

project briefs, project charters, terms of reference, log frames, etcetera, etcetera… which of them comes first? What's the priority if we really are to advise effectively? I think I heard you declare that we have to fine-tune the project charter before we can actually get started on anything helpful, like put in place a management training programme or fire a few supernumerary staff?"

Clovis didn't like Malcolm very much (the sentiment was mutual), so although his questioning was largely meaningless it put Malcolm on the spot, which was something he knew Malcolm particularly did not like. It achieved Clovis's objective of making Malcolm visibly squirm. He looked unutterable things, and puckered up his mouth into something inaudible, but that a lip-reader might indeed have interpreted as 'Oh, just fuck off, will you?'.

"Oh, you must understand that we have to get these things absolutely right, you know. No point in setting out on a complex project if we haven't done the groundwork at the outset. So yes, we need to have agreed on the details of the project brief. Above all, we need evidence – evidence to support the intended outcome of any project, the goals it's intended to achieve…"

"So have you discussed your approach to these things with your main client – the Project Management Division?"

Clovis knew he hadn't, but his aim was to provoke. He was highly scornful of Malcolm's management style, which seemed to him to be based on closeting himself away with his laptop as far removed from all human, let alone client contact, as possible. He was also inclined to sulk if questioned too closely, or if he didn't altogether get his own way, and Clovis was hoping his questioning might bring a sulk on.

"Oh, this is ridiculous," he sneered – predictably –. *"You just don't understand, do you? Those muppets in PMD are totally unprofessional. They haven't a clue about how to put a project brief together…"*

"How do you know that if you haven't actually met up with them?"

"I… well, it's so bloody obvious, isn't it? They haven't a proper professional background, or the first idea about leading consulting projects…"

"Haven't they? I always thought 'leading consulting projects' involved interaction with the client…"

Malcolm goggled and clawed at his glass of beer as if intent on flinging its contents into Clovis' face. Maybe he would have done if Diane hadn't intervened with a typically limp attempt at appeasement:

"I'm sorry, but… I mean, I don't want to be divisive, but actually in this case I think Malcolm may have a point… well, sort of, anyway… I mean, I've met the PMD people myself, and they really don't seem to be all that capable in what they're supposed to do. So, well, maybe it is the best approach to not to get too close to them… sort of, anyway…"

Clovis sniffed and took a swig at his bottle of fizzy beer. Malcolm, who might have been expected to take Diane's intervention as sympathetic, continued to look unutterable things. Diane, poor lamb that she was, had only succeeded in deflecting his contempt towards herself!

"Oh, don't be so pathetic!" he sneered, half-turning towards her. *"A lot of these problems are just down to you anyway – if you hadn't queered the pitch with them at the beginning, confusing them with your muddled ideas and everything, before I came on board with a more structured approach, we wouldn't be having these problems anyway…"*

"Well, I… I'm sorry… I don't think that's quite fair… I mean, well, right from the beginning…"

"I don't care what you think. It's just pathetic. You're all pathetic, all of you. So unprofessional, just so unprofessional."

Malcolm glared around triumphantly, as if he'd just discovered the key to eternal life. Brendyn hummed and hawed a little, and painstakingly examined another spicy chicken wing. Diane simply blushed, and tried to make herself look as small as possible in her uncomfortable Hyatt club armchair.

Such for positive project dynamics!

*

The Lead Consultant

It was lucky for Clovis Buckram that there was another Mr Buckram in the world of international consulting with much the same background as himself, for our Mr Buckram profited very considerably by the other Mr Buckram's name and reputation. In the first place, they were both called Clovis, and in the second place, they were both specialists in human resources management, in different circumstances to be sure, but still they were both in HRM and the mere fact of their being so was very confusing. Added to this, our friend Clovis being of the pushing, self-aggrandising order, he accepted the benefits of the confusion without doubt or hesitation.

We don't mean to insinuate that he went about saying 'I am the celebrated Sir Clovis Buckram KCB, former Deputy Permanent Secretary in Her Majesty's Treasury, President of the International Association of Human Resources Management, board member of various eminent international charitable institutions, etc. etc.'; but if he found he was taken for that Buckram he never troubled to correct the impression. Indeed, if questioned, he would mount the high horse and talk patronisingly of the other Buckram – say he was a decent fellow, if not much of a consultant, and pooh-pooh him considerably. To hear Clovis talk, one would think that he had not only persuaded himself that he was the right Buckram, but that he had made the right Buckram believe so too.

It was also very lucky for Clovis that Damien Driscoll had resigned from Arnaque Consulting before the Trinidad project actually got started, as - *with one exception* - he was the only Arnaque employee who knew for a certainty that the Clovis Buckram the government of Trinidad and Tobago got for its key technical consultant was not the Clovis Buckram (KCB) it thought it was going to get. In writing the

Arnaque proposal for the project, Damien had pulled a trick that he and Clovis had pulled successfully on several occasions previously, in order to win projects with disingenuous governments of developing-country states; namely, colluding in making full play of the KCB, the international charitable institutions etc. to render awestruck the prospective client. After all, who could resist having a bona fide Knight of the Realm on their chosen project team? The fact that Damien was no longer around in this instance gave Clovis a freer hand than he would otherwise have had in mounting the aforementioned high horse. 'After all,' he would say, 'I know our managing partner in the project proposal describes me as a leading management guru in my professional field, a little over the top, perhaps, but not really so very far from the truth. Our managing partner has always been known for the excellence of his judgement of character'.

It is sometimes said that good luck, like London buses and many other things, comes in threes, and the third piece of luck Clovis had in this instance was that his Trinidadian clients didn't question him too much concerning his professional history. Had they done so, they would surely have come to the realisation that C. B., the international consultant was not quite the (K)CB they thought he was. Perhaps they were too in awe of the elements of the KCB reputation; perhaps, if they had an inkling of suspicion, they didn't want to admit it, neither to themselves nor to anyone else who might be interested. This was something, in fact, that our Clovis Buckram had become used to with his clients. After all, who wants to admit they've made a huge mistake and end up looking stupid, a laughing stock? Much better to keep quiet about the matter, go with the flow and hope that everything turns out all right in the end. This approach was considerably helped by Clovis's lofty self-confidence, and a demeanour that threw out a challenge to anyone bold enough to openly doubt the Buckram credentials.

His approach towards the Trinidadians at the dinner they organised for the Arnaque consultant team at the start of the project was a case in point; this at a bijou restaurant in central Port of Spain, with dim lighting, exotic (and expensive) dishes and a clear view across the Queen's Park Savannah.

"An interesting menu," observed Clovis the Magnificent, as he sipped his Chablis during the fish course. "B*ut oh! How sometimes these places get the little details so horribly wrong. I mean, just fancy! They have served up this wine without it being properly iced!"*

"Indeed!" responded their host, the Permanent Secretary, apologetically; this Permanent Secretary being the appointee previous to the one who subsequently gave the consultants such a drubbing in the windowless conference room, and a confirmed Arnaque champion. "*Of course, here in the Caribbean, we are not so savvy about wine as you folks in Europe..."*

"Of course not, of course not… I fully understand," replied Clovis loftily, twirling his glass thoughtfully between his fingers (he had drunk the Chablis, despite its temperature not being up to the mark). "*In point of fact, I touch on the topic of oenology in my latest book 'Putting the Human*

Touch into Human Resources Management' published recently by the Financial Times. These things are more important than one thinks in the context of work/life balance, spiritual well-being, that sort of thing, you know."

"Yes… I'm… I'm sure they are." replied the Permanent Secretary, hesitantly. *"In fact, I'm sure…"*

But Clovis had moved on in his diversionary discourse and wasn't listening.

"Of course, I'd have liked to give you a signed copy of my book, which has had excellent reviews in the professional magazines; but to tell you the truth, I've had the misfortune to lose part of my luggage during my outbound flight; or rather, British Airways have contrived to misplace it. In any event, half my things, including the book haven't yet arrived in Port of Spain."

"How unfortunate, I do hope that…"

"Yes, most unfortunate indeed; not what one would expect when travelling first class as I always do. Not what one would expect at all."

"I suppose you have a good deal of luggage when you come out on these missions?"

"Quite a good deal, yes. I like to ensure I'm well turned out, that sort of thing, out of respect for my clients if for nothing else. Unfortunately, my best three suits have all been declared missing – for now, at least – so I'm afraid you'll only be seeing me in my second-rate rags over the next few days. It really is quite a bore. I don't suppose you could

recommend a good tailor in Port of Spain, could you?"

The Permanent Secretary demurred on this; she hoped the supposed KCB wasn't a degree or two too grand for the humble tasks her ministry needed to be done.

"Anyhow, nothing to be done about it – nothing to be done, just one of those things," continued Clovis loftily. *"Here, take some more wine, before it becomes absolutely too room-temperature to be enjoyed."* And he generously pushed the bottle (which was on the ministry's entertainment expenses bill, like the rest of the meal) towards the PS, thinking that she would want something to wash the lies he was telling her down with.

Brendyn, and the rest of the project team who were seated around the table didn't seek to enlighten the PS and her colleagues concerning the Buckram impudence!

*

Part 3: In Which Things are Going Along Swimmingly: November/December 2014

One of the particularities of the Arnaque Trini project was that it was being paid for directly by the Trini government, rather than via a sponsorship or loan from an agency such as the World Bank or USAid.

This was a reflection of the financial circumstances of Trinidad at the time (2014). As a state with considerable offshore oil reserves and the price of oil then being very high, Trinidad was almost literally awash with money; and the government seemed intent on getting through as much of it as possible, as quickly as possible. If the unemployment rate showed signs of spiking, what could be better than to create a new ministry to take citizens off the streets? If any other sort of problem raised its ugly head in the administration, well, the simplest solution was to initiate a consultancy project to have a look into it and make recommendations, wasn't it? Dozens of projects had started up in this way, many of them drifting aimlessly along without any real intervention from, or benefit to, the client. Officially, the purpose of the Arnaque Consulting project was to have a look at some of these and bring some kind of rationality into it all, as well as (finally) some brake on the colossal spending.

Unfortunately – as Clovis remarked during the bonding session at the Hyatt Hotel – the actual terms of reference for the project, and therefore what the consultants were actually supposed to do, were most unclear, and Brendyn Bryman was not, temperamentally, the kind of man to create order from confusion. As a result, right from the outset the danger was that the project would get sucked into the giant whirlpool of cash disappearing from the Trinidad governmental coffers, rather than make efforts to recover some of the disappearing cash – as it was intended to do.

Clovis observed all of this, some two months into the project, following a rather bad-tempered ride in a taxi from his apartment to the office though the worst of the daily Port of Spain rush hour traffic.

"The fact is", he drawled, *"this government has no notion concerning investment. Take the road network, for example. Over an hour to do the two or so miles from Maraval to the*

centre – an absolute disgrace. They should do something about it – do something about it – rather than invent another pointless ministry. 'The Ministry of Crabs and Coastal Erosion', or something very like, is the latest one, I think – would do more good spent a bit on a decent urban transport system"

Brendyn, who also was in a bad mood that morning, muttered something about the difficulties of civil engineering projects in the context of the problematic topography of Port of Spain.

"What nonsense! I believe there used to be a perfectly workable rail transport system, which was scrapped some time ago… in the early days following independence, I believe. Don't get me wrong, I'm no fan of the old colonial days, not at all – but they managed to get some things right, don't you see?"

Brendyn hummed and hawed consequentially, but by now Clovis was in full flow.

"And anyway, if things are bad enough now, how much worse will they be if the price of oil collapses, as some experts say it will? They've not thought of investing in other sectors of the economy, not at all you know, they'll be high and dry with no revenue coming in and about 96 ministries to service, and complete gridlock in the transport system…."

Brendyn attempted manfully to make his point, but Clovis was no longer listening.

"Oh well, now that I've got here, there's nothing to do in

the project office other than drink tea anyway, so I shall go off to hobnob with those pretty, intelligent girls who make up the Strategic Reform Unit..."

And off he went.

Clovis had a good time with the girls. They took him off at lunchtime to an outdoor concert in the nearby park, and only half of them came back to the office afterwards. Clovis, who did return, installed himself in their open-plan work area (*"much more pleasant than the project office, don't you know – and it's always important to be close to one's client"*) where he spent a pleasant afternoon continuing his hobnobbing and pretending to work on his laptop. Nobody came to disturb him.

*

As any Trini will tell you, 'having fun' constitutes a key element of Trinidadian culture. Hence, perhaps, the lack of rigour concerning sustainable development, infrastructure improvement and consultant project deliverables, etc., all of which kind of things tend to get pushed aside to make way for obligatory entertainment pursuits. Having fun *is indeed* a sort of obligation in Trinidad - it is forced on you, one is *expected* to have fun, even if one isn't really, at least, that's how Clovis would have put it. For example, in his view standing watching a never-ending stream of steel pan performers from a makeshift grandstand in the middle of Queen's Park Savannah, while getting slowly drunk, was very small beer compared with watching thoroughbreds perform from a grandstand at Ascot, Goodwood or wherever (a diversion he tended to extol when he had his KCB hat on).

The steel pan orchestra personnel were taking time off work to do their rehearsals for the carnival coming up in February, and they tended to be – well, rather repetitive, one might say.

The Arnaque consultant team was therefore required by their clients to join them regularly in traditional Trinidadian fun. This included further visits to pan yards to hear orchestras practising; extravagant overnight parties finishing around 7.00 a. m. on the Sunday morning after a night of binge drinking; visits to the Caroni swamp by boat for the Scarlet Ibis (Clovis actually did enjoy this) and other touristic sites. The reactions of the Arnaque team members to these and other entertainments clearly reflected their personalities - Malcolm Shardlow tended to be silently aloof, Diane Willett gawkishly enthusiastic, and Clovis Buckram chattily engaging, even if he wasn't actually enjoying himself that much. As for Brendyn, well, as a Trini himself, he usually adopted the persona of a father figure carefully explaining the hidden meaning of things to his team of consultants, as if they were teenagers out on a school trip. He had the opportunity to do this a lot, as apart from the aforementioned trio there were several other specialist consultants who came in under short-term or local contracts: marketing specialists, procurement specialists, organisational development specialists, all manner of specialists, in fact. Most of them came and went, leaving behind them detailed, well-reasoned and often lengthy reports which, unfortunately, tended not to take much account of each other or the actual needs of the Ministry of Public Administration to do things differently.

Still, all was well. The monthly Arnaque invoices continued to be paid, relations with the MPA staff and management continued to be cordial, and the 'having fun' quotient notched up a gear or two as the Trinidad carnival season came closer. Clovis awaited this with some trepidation.

*

The M&E Specialist and the Project Management Consultant

Diane Willett was not by profession an M&E specialist. She had always been a project administrator – and a very good one – and had worked for Arnaque in this capacity on projects in a number of rather dodgy states – Nigeria, Honduras, South Sudan, Ethiopia – from the latter of which she and all the project team had been expelled with one day's notice by the nasty government for breaching some political protocol.

She had been promoted and appointed to the Trinidad project for her good work performance, and her ability to press on uncomplainingly in difficult circumstances. However, as an M&E specialist she was hopelessly out of her depth.

This was not Diane's fault. Arnaque Consulting was not in the habit of necessarily selecting the best consultant for the job in hand; anyone who was available and whose CV could be tweaked positively to seem an undeniable expert in his or her field would do. Henry Banff, the partner-in-charge who helped Damien Driscoll in writing the Trinidad proposal, thought he was doing Diane a favour sending her to such a plum location, and probably thought if she read a book or two and a few reports about M&E, she would make out OK.

This might well have been the case, had it not been for the rather backbiting nature of the project team. Diane was a large, rather clumsy girl from a farming family, and did indeed resemble a rather gawky farm girl. But despite her lumpy physical presence she was inordinately shy and self-effacing. She simply didn't know how to stand up for herself. Thus, she became a target for some of the more bullying members of the project team – Malcolm Shardlow in particular – and even the generally-genial Brendyn sometimes became ratty with her, through sheer exasperation at her tendency to become flustered and nervously excitable (appearances being all-important in the world of consulting, he felt this didn't go down well with the client).

Eventually, she did indeed show herself up during a client presentation, by mixing up her PowerPoint slides and getting in a tizwoz about it.

Brendyn decided she had to go. Being something of a coward, he didn't want to tell her directly so he deputed Clovis to do it. Reluctantly, Clovis invited her for brunch in a Port of Spain McDonalds one Saturday morning in December to break the bad news.

After some initial pleasantries, Clovis came to the point.

"Ah well… the fact is, Diane, Brendyn asked me to have a word or two with you. Would have done it himself of course, but apparently he is away from Port of Spain this weekend,

and may not be back until mid-next week..."

He glanced at Diane sideways, 'she must know what's coming,' he thought to himself, 'but she doesn't look too miserable about it'. He was encouraged to carry on.

"You see, the project being in the state it is, Brendyn's view is that we no longer really need an M&E specialist. So it may be that you'll be returning to London at the end of next week..."

Diane looked relieved if anything, as indeed she was. The PowerPoint fiasco had been the last straw for her as well as for Brendyn, and she was mightily glad to be presented with such an easy way out. She demurred a little purely as a matter of form, but they both knew this was just a matter of consultancy *politesse.*

After a few minutes' discussion about the practicalities of it all, Clovis finished his coffee and Egg McMuffin, parted company from Diane and wandered back up the road to his nearby apartment overlooking the Savannah. Things turned out very well for Diane in the end. Henry Banff was quite a kindly man and offered her a post in administration in the Arnaque head office in the City of London. This suited her much better, professionally and temperamentally, than the hotbed of front-line consulting.

*

Malcolm Shardlow, Diane's chief tormentor in Trinidad, was quite a nasty piece of work. Youngish, rather tall and willowy, he acquired among some of his colleagues the rather disparaging nickname of 'the human hairpin'.

However, unlike a hairpin, there was nothing bendable about Malcolm. He was the most strait-laced, narrow-minded, standoffish individual imaginable, with a high opinion of almost nothing except himself. He had married a Chinese lady, and again the unkind amongst his colleagues sometimes said that only an uncomplainingly submissive Chinese woman (according to the stereotypes) could have stood him.

Clovis' jibes at the Hyatt about Malcolm never meeting his client counterparts were actually perfectly true. The Arnaque team had been allocated two adjacent project offices in the ministry building, and whenever he could, Malcolm closeted himself away in the vacant room with his laptop-full of project management tools, and rarely came out. Nobody knew what exactly what he was up to. He didn't even bother to greet his colleagues when he arrived at the office in the morning.

Naturally, this rendered Malcolm rather unpopular among several of his colleagues, Clovis and Brendyn included. They tended to not speak to each other very much, which of course was rather a problem. What was more of a problem was that Malcolm, who at bottom was rather naive and immature, fell under the influence of Josie, the Trinidadian Marketing Consultant who joined the project mid-way through.

Josie was quite a schemer, and it seemed to her that there was no sense in the ministry employing all these foreign consultants when there were plenty of Trinidadians available like her who (in her opinion at least) could do the work just as well. She quickly spotted that Malcolm was not on terms with most of the others and decided to make use of him to further her own ends. Pretty soon, it was that Malcolm withdrew almost completely from intercourse with his Project Leader and others, and went off on his own to do things that Josie had suggested to him but that had nothing at all to do with the work plan.

The upshot of this was the formation of a cabal of Josie, a couple of other Trinidadian consultants and Malcolm, who set themselves up to undermine the efforts of the others and take over their work wherever possible. For quite some time they got away with this, as Brendyn, not the most observant of project managers, simply did not notice what was happening. When he did finally twig, he blew his top and stormed into the adjacent project office where Malcolm had installed himself as usual, to confront him. He would have preferred to have things out with Josie directly, but as she was on very good terms with the PS, he thought it best not to.

Malcolm's first instinct was to treat Brendyn's verbal tirade with cold disdain. This only enraged Brendyn further, who grabbed Malcolm by the throat and pushed him off his revolving office chair.

"I'll be having a long conversation with Henry about you! I don't want you on this project team anymore! I don't know what you've been doin' in here all these weeks, but it's comin' to an end right now! And you can hand over all your project files, you slimy little creep!"

This was not normal project manager behaviour, but Brendyn was truly beside himself. He had known for a long time that things weren't going too well, he was worried about what might happen next, and the revelations about Malcolm sent him over the edge.

Malcolm picked himself up off the carpet, shaking slightly; whether with anger or fear, we cannot say.

"Well, I'm sorry you feel that way," he lisped, *"but you've only yourself to blame. This project is a complete mess, and you know it..."*

"Yes, a complete mess because of jerks like you! The Deputy PS came to see me yesterday. He's your main client counterpart, if that means anything to you. Not one report! He's had nothing from you, in fact hardly ever even seen you, in the last three months..."

Malcolm drew himself up to his not inconsiderable full height and looked down his nose at Brendyn.

"I don't work with people who are unprofessional. I know I can help them, of course, but they wouldn't understand my methods, so I'm obliged to do things my own way. Josie understands all this. Unfortunately, you, and quite a few of the others, simply don't."

Brendyn resisted the temptation to grab Malcolm by the throat again and this time give him a full licking. Instead, with a snort of anger, he turned away and marched out of the room, slamming the door behind him.

*

Brendyn's Skype conversation with Henry Banff didn't help

him very much. Henry was very much the palliative sort, and he persuaded Brendyn not to kick Malcolm out of the door 'in the interests of project harmony, don't you know – project harmony'. 'If only he knew how things are!' reflected Brendyn, who was beginning by now to despair about the project, wishing himself back in a nice, comfortable marketing role in the City of London, or something.

*

Part 4: In which Everything Falls Apart: January 2015

If, as we mentioned earlier, good luck is sometimes said to come in batches of three; well, bad luck can equally be said to do so. This was in fact the case with the Arnaque project, and was cumulatively the cause of the project coming crashing down at the beginning of 2015 – just before the real start of the carnival season which Clovis had been so dubiously anticipating.

The first slice of bad luck might have been anticipated – indeed it *was* anticipated by Clovis as per his previous remarks on the issue, and by many others – the price of oil on world markets plummeted by 70 percent, one of the biggest falls in modern history. Indeed, it was probably not the fall itself but the massive scale of it that caught the government of Trinidad and Tobago napping. The impact was immediate and drastic. Shock! Horror! Ministries had to *share* their post-Christmas staff parties with other ministries, rather than 'going it alone'! The traditional distribution of presents to staff was rather underwhelming compared with the norm (consultants were also included:

Clovis appropriately received a small wine carafe). Overall, the scale of all-important entertainment activities was drastically reduced, the normally highly festive pre-carnival spirit was sorely dampened by fears for the future. More materially, ministries sought ways to wriggle out of or otherwise terminate most of the many consulting projects they had on-running, for which termination the Arnaque project was a prime candidate.

The second was that the Permanent Secretary of the Ministry of Public Administration, who had commissioned the Arnaque project and had always been a staunch defender of it against all charges that it wasn't achieving very much, was replaced by a new Permanent Secretary; the same, in fact, who was friendly with Josie and who ultimately gave the Arnaque team such a hard time in the ministry's conference room. The Arnaque supporter was shuffled sideways into a non-existent ministry – a sort of Permanent Secretary without portfolio – while the new one, who was much more hard-nosed, began her reign by investigating all the ministry's ongoing projects with the help of the Deputy Permanent Secretary – who had never been an Arnaque fan in the first place. The result was that the Permanent Secretarial Eye of Sauron soon lighted on the project files and found them seriously wanting – plenty of measured recommendations, plenty of eye-catching diagrams and pie-charts, but little in the way of concrete advice. It must be said that the new Permanent Secretary was rather predisposed against Arnaque anyway, but reading their reports only hardened her resolve to cut away from them if she could. A quick calculation of the money that had been spent, and the money still outstanding in the project budget, hardened this resolve further.

The third piece of bad luck: well, one afternoon Clovis was again installed in the Strategic Planning Unit's open-plan work area, when the Personal Assistant to the new PS came wandering over with a tall, middle-aged, bespectacled and clearly Caribbean-origin man in tow. Clovis, who was again indulging himself in a game of Freecell on his laptop, hastily closed it down and switched over to a backup window with some complex Excel tables in conspicuous display, which he always had open in case of such interruptions.

"Ah, here you are," the PA said, *"been lookin' for you all over the office. This is Doctor Dexter Grantville, who was the Deputy Prime Minister of Grenada before he retired a few years ago. Now he's been appointed our Strategic Adviser by the PS, and he's been brought in to help her look through the ongoing work portfolio and make some recommendations."*

Clovis didn't particularly like the sound of this, so he thought he had better be super polite. As usual in such circumstances, his first instinct was to mount his high KCB horse and patronise the former Deputy Prime Minister mercilessly. But he didn't get the chance.

"Very glad to meet you." put in the doctor with a smile, before Clovis could draw breath. *"I've been hearin' quite a lot about the work you Arnaque folks have been doin'. Critical stuff, critical stuff, indeed."*

And the doctor proffered Clovis his hand. He was very talkative and friendly. After a few more pleasantries, he continued,

"Anyhow, must let you get on with your work, I guess. Where can I find your Lead Consultant? I was told he'd be around here somewhere..."

Up to this point Clovis had not managed to get a word in edgeways, so he hadn't introduced himself. Now, at last, he smiled suavely and offered Doctor Dexter his hand.

"Actually… well, yes, that's me. I'm the Lead Consultant on the Arnaque project. Honoured to meet you, I'm sure, Doctor. And in point of fact..."

Clovis paused, sensing the doctor looked rather discomfited.

"Beg pardon," he said, *"but I thought the Lead Consultant was Clovis Buckram."*

"Buckram it is," replied Clovis, yawning and stretching out his arms as if to show the doctor what a great man he had to contend with.

"But not the Sir Clovis Buckram I met at the Commonwealth Leaders' Forum in London two years ago..."

If Doctor Dexter had put a pistol to our friend's head, he could not have given him a greater shock; all the lies he had served up to the Trinidadians, either hinting at or openly proclaiming his KCB credentials, came back to him in awful clarity. He tried to bluster his way out – yes, there was indeed another Clovis Buckram doing the rounds, who was quite a good sort of fellow, certainly a KCB and very eminent but not really suited to the type of work required by this project, etc., etc. - and to a certain extent he succeeded, leaving the good doctor still very amiable but slightly puzzled by it all. Clovis hoped he wouldn't let on. But he noticed that in parting the PA gave him a rather old-fashioned look. Altogether he didn't see how the cat could not be let out of the bag, and started to make provisions accordingly.

And so it proved. Doctor Grantville of necessity was in close contact with the Permanent Secretary, and it was not long before the whole truth was known to her and to all the other senior managers of the Ministry of Public Administration. Before the week was out, an urgent Skype discussion was requested with Henry Banff (who happened to know perfectly well all about the Clovis Buckram deception: indeed, it was he who had carefully written it into the project proposal in ambiguous terminology).

"Well, Mr Banff. I hope you're keeping well. I'll come straight to the point. The government is mindful to terminate the contract with Arnaque Consulting, as you know the government finances have taken a severe blow and we urgently need to make economies..."

Even hard-nosed Trinidadians like the Permanent Secretary can be scrupulously polite. Banff tried to demur, but by now the PS was emboldened and had the bit firmly between her teeth.

"I know, Mr Banff, this news must come as something of a shock to you. I'm sorry about that. But, you must know also, I've been looking through your reports with my Strategic Adviser, and I must say that we are not... ah... altogether

satisfied with some of your team's progress. I'm really sorry, but my Adviser has been reviewing some of the finer points of the contract documents, and it really is within our rights to bring things to an immediate end. Of course, I will discuss all of this with your Project Manager and the rest of the team. But please take it from me that the necessary steps will be put in motion, of course you will be paid in full for the time your consultants have spent with us up to today's date..."

We draw a veil over some of the juicier elements of the discussion that followed. Suffice it to say that the little scene in the conference room, as described in part 1, occurred very shortly after; and not long after *that,* all the expatriate Arnaque team members were back on BA flights out of Port of Spain.

All the team members, that is, except Malcolm Shardlow, who, completely besotted, had abandoned his Chinese wife and taken up with Josie, with whom he had formed a harmonious relationship during their joint effort to undermine completely the Arnaque initiative. As Clovis Buckram acidly remarked,

"Well, I just hope they can make each other happy. If they're speaking to each other, that would be a start at least: the human hairpin was never much of a hand at congenial conversation."

The Clovis Conversations

Conversation Number 1: The Spaceman

My good friend Clovis Buckram likes his comforts, and when organising his professional travels usually manages to negotiate contracts allowing him to take business class flights.

"After all," he has declared, "there are just so many irritations and uncertainties surrounding international travel; one simply *must do what one can* to limit them as much as possible, you know. Ugh! I can think of nothing worse than being squashed for a long period of time into that ever-more-constricted space that constitutes 'economy class' nowadays, in one of those long, thin metal tubes manufactured either by Boeing or Airbus. It really is quite a horrible prospect."

And Clovis indeed shudders with horror and rolls his eyes at the appalling thought, so much his sensibilities are jolted just by the idea of the thing.

"You know, Kram, sometimes, I feel rather like a spaceman must feel. Not that I've ever been jetted into space, of course… but I'm frequently jetted into obscure parts of planet Earth, spending long periods of time en route, and not having a clue what I'll find when I get there..."

I can empathise fully with Clovis – the more so as, not being as good a negotiator as he is, I often *do* have to travel economy class. Although, like him, my missions are all terrestrial. I think for many people, if I told them my next consulting project was on Mars, they wouldn't really be surprised. Take my mother-in-law for instance, she's getting old and rather scatterbrained now, and anyway she's never really shown much interest in my professional travels. She would probably just say, *'Oh, really?'* and carry on thinking about something else. I don't really blame her. Hmmm... Mars might be quite interesting, I'm sure the Martians could benefit from some advice from a battle-scarred international adviser like me. But back to Clovis, who has more skill than I do in putting across his sentiments.

"...*What do I mean* when I say I feel like a spaceman, I hear you ask? Well, as I said, there's the unknown. I suspect that spacemen have similar trepidations, you know, when they are about to set out on a new mission - apprehension, a little excitement, a desire to do well. And like a spaceman, I know there'll be unexpected problems along the way, that I'm going to have to solve on my own. Oh, I might be able to send a message back to mission control to get some help, but in the end, it's almost certainly going to be down to me to sort things out when they start going wrong, as they so frequently do."

Knowing Clovis as I do, I have full confidence in his ability to extricate himself from such problems and difficulties as do occur, with the minimum of fuss and discomfort. In my case, well, frequently there have been considerable discomforts both moral and physical, but somehow I too have always managed to overcome them and get back to 'Planet Massigne'* in one piece, although with considerably less aplomb than Clovis. Here are some of those I remember most.

* The Rednip residence being Village de Massigne, Loire Atlantique, France

Kicking my Heels in Kigali

Well, Clovis, it was like this. I was working in Burundi some years ago, and travelling between Bujumbura and Planet Massigne could sometimes be a little tricky. It usually involved a flight from Nantes to Amsterdam, then Amsterdam to Nairobi, then connection with the Kenya Airways' 'Bermuda Triangle' flight going on the route Nairobi – Bujumbura – Kigali and back again. Making the connection on the way back at Nairobi was often quite a scramble, if there was any kind of delay.

On one occasion, waiting at Bujumbura, the incoming flight <u>was</u> delayed about an hour. My blood pressure started rising a little, but we made up a bit of time continuing to Kigali. Things were looking (relatively) good.

We took off from Kigali, I breathed a sigh of relief and settled down in my seat. Ten minutes later we were back on the tarmac again – in Kigali. A technical problem with the plane, the pilot had turned round and gone back.

The big difficulty with this was that I was stranded at a different place from the one I had started from. It was also late at night, so there were few people around inside the terminal. You need a visa to enter Rwanda and the visa booth was closed. Therefore I, along with a small number of other travellers, was stuck. A Kenya Airways' official did eventually turn up, but she wandered off with some vague promises that she would sort things out. I wasn't very optimistic, knowing that in situations like this, a Kenyan's inclination is to tell you what they think you want to hear, rather than what actually is happening. I managed to buy a drink, and talked in French to my fellow stranded travellers, one of whom was a young priest who was getting very upset at the prospect of missing some ecumenical event or other. Eventually we somehow managed to get leave to exit the terminal, and after another longish wait for the release of our luggage – which was still stuck inside somewhere else – were bussed off to a hotel for the night.

"A reasonable standard hotel, I trust? After all, Kenya Airways are in bed with Air France/KLM, aren't they? And I've been given to understand that Kigali is quite a developed place now, you know, not just through all the international aid but quite a vibrant economy in its own right..."

Yes, if I remember correctly, it was a decent enough hotel, but as I arrived there in the wee small hours I didn't notice much about my surroundings, I just wanted to get to bed. Didn't sleep well. Back to the airport as early as possible next morning, found someone in the Kenya Airways office who printed off documents for me for the next flight back to Nairobi and on to Amsterdam ... so onwards I went. The terminal at Nairobi was packed with angry and frustrated travellers, the Easter break was coming up and Kenya Airways clearly had major logistical problems... as you know, even at the best of times Nairobi Airport is pretty horrible, just a long row of dusty shops selling the same souvenirs, a few plastic chairs, a tawdry cafeteria. When I tried to check in for Amsterdam, the KLM officials looked askance at the boarding pass I'd been issued in Kigali, and made me hang around at the back of the departure lounge. I'd had my doubts with it, it had just seemed too easy to get it in the first place, but I was too fagged out to argue about it.

"You mean... the KA official at Kigali was a fake? A boarding pass is a boarding pass, in my humble experience..."

Well, I never found out about that. Anyway, after another quite long, nervous wait, those kind KLM people let me onto their flight. One of my last images of Nairobi was of the French priest, almost in tears, pleading with the official at the transfer desk to put him on a flight to anywhere within the next two days. He hadn't been as lucky as me!

"Yes, didn't you think of trying the business lounge? I mean, it isn't much better than the common departure area at Nairobi, but at least you can get a drink of some sort, and relax a little in what passes for a comfy chair... oh, but of course, I suppose you weren't business class? You really should <u>insist</u> on your clients upgrading you, you know..."

Yes, I do know. Clovis, you're absolutely right, as usual. Spending hours and hours sitting on a plastic chair in an airline terminal, even spending the whole night on (or under) a plastic chair, is not very pleasant at all. Unfortunately, it's something I have experienced on more than one occasion...

Benighted in Belgrade

I had a premonition something would go wrong when the taxi taking me to the airport got a puncture. The driver fixed it pretty quickly so I arrived in plenty of time, but I realised there was a problem as soon as I got inside the terminal building. Hundreds and hundreds of people, just milling about; all the departure boards showing all flights leaving at 2.00 p. m. – in about two hours' time. *Whatever* was going on?

A strike by Serbian Airlines, *that's* what was going on. And my flight back to Paris was with Serbian. As for the departure boards – well, when 2.00 p. m. came around, they simply flipped all the departures round to 4.00 p. m. Clearly, getting out of Serbia was going to require some creative thinking...

"Well, it must have been a problem – of course I can see that. But there are other airlines flying out of Belgrade, aren't there? Why didn't you just book yourself onto another flight?"

Of course, Clovis, that's what I should have done. I suppose I was somehow hoping Serbian Airlines would sort things out and get moving again. So I waited around, like everyone else. The departure boards flipped round to 6.00 p. m. Eventually I gave up and took the courtesy bus back into Belgrade. Just as in Kigali, a night in an anonymous hotel – this time a typically Eastern European one, stuck in a 1970s time warp, definitely not 'reasonable standard', but at least a (rather narrow) bed for the night...

"Really, Kram, I'm disappointed with you. You can be such a wimp, at times. You should have asserted yourself more – given them to understand at the airport that they had an unavoidable obligation to get you home with a different airline, and that you would accept nothing other than immediate redress. If you'd just bullied them a little, of course they would have caved in. They always do."

You may be right. Anyway, next morning, bus back to the airport, no sign of any activity at the Serbian Airlines counter, so I booked a rather expensive flight home with Lufthansa, via Frankfurt. Fortunately, I was being paid generous fees for this assignment, so in the end, the cost didn't matter too much.

"Oh really – that's beside the point, you know, completely beside the point. If you'd been more assertive in the first place, things would have been sorted out much more satisfactorily. And anyway – booking your flights with Serbian Airlines: well, what can you expect?"

Yes, I suppose so. I remember, while waiting in the crowded departure lounge in Frankfurt for my onwards flight, a Lufthansa official coming round and offering passengers two days' accommodation in a hotel, plus a cash bonus, if they agreed to delay their journey for two days. The flight was overbooked. I kept my head down and pretended not to notice, but a young couple sitting nearby accepted the offer and were ushered out, smiling, their hotel vouchers in hand...

Stuffed in Sierra Leone

"Sierra Leone! What a place that must be! Even worse than Burundi, I should imagine. You really do take on some strange assignments, Mr Kram Rednip..."

Well actually, Sierra Leone is not too bad, I rather enjoyed my brief sojourn there of about three weeks. It had a very 1960s feel. Nothing seemed to have been updated or renovated, despite the fact that it is rich in mineral wealth.

The big mining companies did not seem to have moved in – not to Freetown, at least. I never got to go back, as the Ebola crisis hit hard, curtailing all development activity for several years.

However - my strong message to anyone travelling to Sierra Leone – don't arrive at nighttime.

The simple reason for this is that Freetown Airport is not in Freetown, but the other side of a very wide estuary. The only way across the estuary is by ferry, or a very long drive up the estuary to the nearest bridge, then down the other side. Neither is a possibility after dark.

"I'm sure I read somewhere that there was a helicopter service from the airport – not that I'm thinking of ever going to Freetown, you understand?"

Not anymore – there used to be – but more than one of the (Russian built) helicopters crashed en route, so the service was discontinued on safety grounds. Anyway, as I was saying, no service after dark, and although I was met at the airport by my client counterpart, by the time I cleared immigration it *was* just about dark. Most of the other passengers, who presumably knew the score, had long since cleared off to Freetown on the last ferry. So – another long, uncomfortable sojourn on an airport standard issue plastic chair.

Eventually, very early in the morning, my counterpart negotiated passage on a small speedboat to take us across. Apart from the boatman, my counterpart and me, there was only one other passenger, a youngish woman who seemed rather nervous.

"Nervous! Well, I'm not surprised at that. Also rather fagged out I should imagine, if she too had spent a jolly time overnight at the airport terminal..."

Yes, Clovis, exactly so. The speedboat journey was certainly invigorating, bouncing along atop the dirty brown waves of the estuary until we reached halfway across, at which point the outboard motor cut out. I think by this time I was too weary to really be nervous myself. Anyway, the boatman, who didn't seem too concerned, reached down over the back and fished up several long strands of weeds that had snagged the propeller. A few pulls on the starter rope and the motor sputtered into life again. What relief! After that, although the outboard threatened to cut out again a couple of times, we made it over to Freetown without further incident.

"Interesting. Reminds me of a time I was in Guyana a few years ago, and took a speedboat across the estuary of the Essequibo to some ecology camp or other. A nice, placid journey out, but the journey back...! The wind had got up and the waves were just enormous. The boatman handed out oilskins to all his passengers, and we soon found out why. I think we spent more time bouncing into the spray just above the waves, rather than crashing through them. Quite invigorating – and, I must confess, a little scary."

After my own experience of estuarine speedboating, I can imagine. Anyway, my mission in Sierra Leone went quite well, but I had further problems getting out of the country again. Not with the boat trip this time – a much bigger, more stable vessel was provided – but due to torrential rain in Liberia the return flight was delayed several hours. More plastic chair misery, missed flight in Casablanca but put on a later one, overnight at an Accor Hotel at Orly… all fairly typical of the problems of (space) travel!

Very long way to Vanuatu

"Now, Vanuatu sounds much more my sort of ticket. A very interesting place, I'm told, although of course rather a long journey to get there? You were afforded business class for this one at least, I trust?"

Well, actually no, Clovis. I hang my head in shame in saying this. The problem is, you know, the European Union has such strict rules concerning consultants' travel arrangements. They did allow me a couple of paid days per trip, however, by way of compensation…

"Economy class? All I can say is that I'm floored, I really am. And of course, from the EU's point of view, it's so counterproductive. What's the sense in sending an expert literally right across the world, if he's going to be too worn out to do anything properly? I ask you!"

I couldn't agree more. In fact, I travelled to Vanuatu twice: the first time for a period of four weeks – so I had plenty of time to recover from the journey: the second time for just two days. That was the EU's planned schedule, so that's how it had to be. It really does show up the stupid inflexibility of the European Union at times.

"I find it difficult to believe I'm hearing this. How long does it take to get to Vanuatu from Europe? Thirty-six hours?

Two days? So you travelled for two days there and two days back, to spend just two days in situ? Mad - completely mad!"

Again, I couldn't agree more. But let me tell you about my first trip, which I enjoyed very much. The project I was involved in was for the Ministry of Agriculture, and required quite a lot of internal travel between several of the islands that make up the Vanuatu archipelago, accompanied by a 'minder' (sometimes two). A lot of what I got up to (in between work activities – promise!) was very touristic, including a trip to the top of an active volcano, indulging in local specialities such as mud crab and kava, participating in Melanesian food rituals, visiting pristine beaches and farming communities in the remote hinterlands, and witnessing the ritualistic resolution of a trade dispute between Vanuatu and the Solomon Islands. All of this, and more, made for an unforgettable experience of life in a place geographically and geopolitically way, way out of the mainstream. Oh yes, and then there was the time…

"Thank you, thank you, Kram, I get the picture, very distinctly, very invigorating I must say. But what about your second trip? I mean, how did you <u>cope</u> with what must have been, to use common parlance, a 'punishing schedule'?"

It involved a good deal of mental preparation. Since at least three flights were required to get there, as well as a train journey to Paris, from a mental perspective I simply separated each leg of the trip into 'bite-sized chunks' as the saying goes. Then throughout the gruelling schedule I kept doing little mental calculations concerning what percentage of the overall journey had been accomplished, and what percentage there still was to go, things like that. Anything I could to keep myself sane. Fortunately, all the connections worked OK, everything went pretty much according to plan. And jetlag wasn't too much of a problem, I guess I was so keyed-up to complete my mission it didn't kick in at all. Not until the end of the trip back, at least. I remember falling asleep standing up on the train back home from Paris, there not being any seats available!

"Nevertheless – rather you than me: I certainly wouldn't have stood for it. Your mission was, at least, a success, I hope?"

Yes, kind of. I had to deliver a one-day training course to some ministry officials, and although it went well enough, I don't think they were actually all that interested. And I always suspected that the main motivation of my counterpart was to get some free travel around the islands, relax a little, maybe scope out the possibilities for some personal business opportunities in a few places - though maybe I'm being a bit churlish in stating this. He was very friendly and helpful, after all, and *did* provide some fascinating things to see and do.

"Well, I'm glad at least you got something of a good time out of it. After all, if one really must become a terrestrial spaceman, one should be entitled to a few little pleasures from it."

There usually *are* a few pleasures, as you know, Clovis: memorable events, places visited, things seen, things learned, stuff like that. But now I've *finished* my professional travels, I can't say I miss them very much. In fact, the thought of another long-haul flight (even business class!) fills me with horror. I'm much happier staying on Planet Massigne, doing my garden, playing my piano or whatever, and simply *reminiscing* about my interplanetary adventures!

Conversation Number Two: What is Intelligence?

"Human intelligence? Well, it's an almost indefinable concept, you know. Hardly any two psychologists can agree on a common definition. The one that seems most apt to me is that of David Wechsler: 'the capacity to act purposefully, to think rationally, and to deal effectively with one's environment'. But there are so many others. It really is very confusing."

"And yet, Clovis, it's usually fairly easy to discern whether a particular person is intelligent or not, isn't it? It's generally pretty apparent from the outset."

"That's why I think the Wechsler definition – which is based on behaviour 'within one's environment' rather than any artificial test, which necessarily can only measure a fairly limited set of mental abilities – is one of the best. And I don't know exactly how it works, of course, but I'm sure I personally would score extremely high on the Wechsler Adult Intelligence Scale, very high indeed compared to the average."

"Yes Clovis, of course, I'm sure you would. (Thinks: you would certainly score extremely well on the Wechsler Adult Impudence Scale, if nothing else.) Perhaps you should think of becoming a member of MENSA. I'm sure taking *their* test would be child's play for someone like you."

"Oh really, I couldn't be bothered with any of that stuff. I really don't see the point. From what I've heard about MENSA, it's just a singles club for a bunch of geeks to play three-dimensional chess with each other and congratulate each other on being so much brighter than everyone else."

******

Clovis may be right, but I suspect the real reason he hasn't tried the MENSA test is that he's secretly afraid he might fail, and not get in after all. Being able to declare himself to be one of the most intelligent 2% of human beings on the planet is surely something that would appeal to his lofty sense of self-esteem, otherwise... but we'll let it pass.

We have only ever encountered one person, in our whole life, who professed to being a member of MENSA. P**** B*** was not in the same league as Clovis in terms of impudence, but he probably was in terms of self-esteem. He was actually quite an amiable fellow – always willing to do helpful things for any of his friends – but there was a certain sense of detachment about him, which somehow said 'I'm different from all the rest of you. My cognitive powers are such that they are well beyond your comprehension: I do what I can to tolerate you from my lofty standpoint'. It was as if we, his friends, were a group of children who needed guiding and humouring. It could be quite irritating at times, especially when, as was frequently the case, he declared his MENSA credentials as in some way justifying his undeniable air of intellectual superiority.

Despite the intellectual superiority, P**** sometimes did some rather stupid things. He had got married at a quite early age, to a young woman who, besides being rather frumpy, could never have been described as highly intelligent, under any definition of the term. It was hard to understand why P**** had married her in the first place. Maybe he thought he was doing her a favour, or maybe it was just as a result of one of the wild bouts of enthusiasm to which he was frequently prone. In any event, by the time we became acquainted with him (in our late 20s, we believe) he had become completely irritated by her. He tended to ignore her completely most of the time, which could be a little awkward during social gatherings, although she herself didn't seem to mind too much. She was so mousey and self-effacing, most of the time it was difficult to notice she was actually there.

Things, however, came to a head during a vacation in Rome. P****, who had some Italian ancestry, rented an apartment in the centre of town one summer, and generously invited his friends (including us) to pass some time there. We had a very good time in Rome – first time we had ever been there, in fact – but the lack of rapport between P**** and – we forget what her name was – was even more embarrassing than before. 'Ignoring her' now meant simply leaving her to her own devices, so while P**** went off exploring the Eternal City she was quite often left alone in the apartment all day. Again, she didn't seem to mind too much, but by now P**** frequently indulged in offhand or snide remarks about her, and it was evident that a divorce would not be far away. The culmination of all this came when, somewhere in Rome, P**** chanced upon a young Israeli woman who, to the rest of us, seemed more than anything to display the tendencies of a terrorist. P****, however, was completely besotted, bouncing around her like an excited puppy and frequently making unflattering comparisons between her and his wife. Fortunately, the terrorist was not very responsive, so nothing came of it except, perhaps, the acceleration of the divorce that would inevitably have happened anyway.

"There, you see, these MENSA types, they aren't really all that intelligent after all, are they? Not under my preferred definition, at least. But your fellow, I imagine, fancied himself as some sort of mathematical genius, and worked as a computer programmer or something, I suppose?"

"Well yes, Clovis, you're just about right, as far as I can remember, he was a whizz at maths and worked in computers."

"There you have it, then – there you have it – these so-called 'intelligence tests', the IQ Test and so on and so forth, they're very narrow in what they actually measure. Intelligence is much broader in scope and takes many forms. I don't suppose people like Shakespeare, or van Gogh, were any good at maths, but no one could deny they were geniuses."

It occurred to us that we had read an article a few days before, concerning 'the most gifted child in Britain'. What Clovis said struck a chord – this particular child was phenomenally gifted at maths, and was going up to Oxford at the age of eight, or something, to be the marvel of his tutors and take a quadruple first class Honours Degree in advanced mathematics with a couple of postgraduate degrees in quantum physics thrown in for good measure, all within a matter of a few months. But how would he make out in adult life? The article went on to consider the careers of previous 'most gifted child' nominees: again, all mathematical wizards, but who tended for all their brilliance to settle into fairly ordinary adult careers – as teachers at secondary schools, rather typically.

"Again, all this only goes to prove my point further. Being gifted at maths is really no more noteworthy than being gifted at something else: creative writing, painting, even cricket or football. No more noteworthy, and certainly not a guarantee of success in life. It's just as I said earlier: 'thinking rationally and making good choices in your environment', that's the <u>real</u> measure of intelligence."

"Again, I agree, Clovis - almost. Not sure about the cricket and football, though."

"No? Well think about it a little. A footballer who's regarded as 'intelligent', for example, who can always be in the right place at the right time, who can play the perfect pass into the perfect space and who can 'read the game', as the saying goes. His environment is the football pitch, and his thought processes and decision-making <u>within</u> that environment, taking account of physics, his knowledge of his own team and the opposition, the complex tactical manoeuvres during the game aimed at creating an advantage – don't they require as much skill as someone who understands complex mathematical problems?"

Clovis sniffed and looked smug, so sure was he of his point.

"I suppose so, although obviously he is operating in a very narrow physical environment..."

"Perhaps so, but is it any more restricted than the environment of the gifted mathematician? As you pointed out, your friend P**** was not so adept at solving problems in the real world as he was at writing computer programmes now, was he?"

"No, that he wasn't."

Clovis was warming to his theme now.

"Anyway, talking about 'child geniuses', do you think we are really doing them a service by singling them out as 'special' in this way? You know more about children than me – having fathered one or two – but I can only recoil in horror at the thought of labelling little Ronnie or little Lucy as 'gifted', sometimes when they're barely out of the nappy stage. Can't do much for their prospects of integrating with others. Much better to let them think of themselves as normal, so they can go on and lead normal lives, even if they <u>are</u> *in some way different. Their parents should think carefully about these things, you know."*

"Oh, Clovis, you have a point, certainly, you have a point."

We cast our mind back, once again to our friend P****. Shortly after his divorce, he married again, this time to a young woman who, though probably nowhere near as intelligent as he was (in his mind at least), was clearly on a more even footing with the P**** personality than wife number1 had ever been. Within a year or so she gave birth to a baby, and not too long afterwards – indeed, when the little one <u>was</u> barely out of nappy stage – he (or she, can't remember which) was voted 'gifted' by P****, on what grounds we know not, but probably simply because he assumed transmission of MENSA-quality genes by himself had unquestioningly taken place.

We can't help feeling that the 'gifted child' status bestowed by P**** on his firstborn was more important for his own self-esteem than for anything else. We can only hope the little one has survived the experience, and has managed to carve out a normal adult life for him (or her) self, whether gifted or not. We leave the last words to Ian Dury:

> *There ain't half been some clever bastards*
> *(lucky bleeders, lucky bleeders)*
> *There ain't half been some clever bastards.*

> *Van Gogh did some eyeball pleasers*
> *He must have been a pencil squeezer.*
> *He didn't do the Mona Lisa*
> *That was an Italian geezer.*

Conversation Number Three: To Be or Not to Be (Gay)

By now, Clovis the Magnificent was in full flow.

"You know, one thing that considerably irritates me is the way the adjective 'gay' has been appropriated by what is now commonly referred to as the *'LGBT Community'. In former days, up until quite recently in fact, it signified 'light-hearted and carefree'; or, in relation to colour, dazzling or very bright. It had a myriad of nuances and interpretations, and was used as such by poets, artists, great thinkers. Now*

it merely indicates a specific sexual orientation. What a sorry fate for a word originally so descriptive, so vibrant, so polyvalent!"

And Clovis sighed resignedly, while finishing off his glass of what would perhaps, in former days, have been described as 'one of the gay, carefree wines of 'Old France'.

"I'm sure you're right, Clovis, but one can't prevent these things from happening, can one? After all, language is not set in stone. It follows trends, it adapts to the changing values and attitudes of successive generations. Who knows that a hundred years from now, the term 'gay' will not once again be associated with lightness of spirit, or brightness, or *joie de vivre*?"

Clovis adopted a pensive attitude, while refilling his glass with two hundred millilitres of the sparkling, gay fluid that brought so much *joie de vivre* to <u>his</u> carefree soul.

"Ah, there, you see, you've brought me round to deploring something else, that causes me <u>considerable</u> mental torment when I reflect upon it: the artificial manipulation of language. It just <u>can't be done.</u> Take the French language, for example. Despite the attempts of that august institution, 'L'Academie Française' to ban Anglo-Saxonisms from 'La Langue Française', the creeping growth of terms like 'hashtag', and 'business', or even 'vintage' - even within public bodies - cannot be prevented. And personally, I don't think it should. I ask you! Why should an institution founded under Louis XIII in 1635, and whose members still wear lace-bedizened hats and jewel-encrusted swords in demonstration of their intellectual superiority over

everyone else, be able to decide what the French hoi polloi should and shouldn't say? Nonsensical – quite nonsensical, say I."

"But Clovis, aren't you arguing against yourself, here? If the term 'gay' has come to mean something different in common speech from its original meaning, isn't that just the normal process of linguistic evolution?"

Clovis twirled his glass between his fingers, then swallowed its contents and reached for another refill.

"Well, I s'pose you're right, s'pose you're right. P'raps I shouldn't get so upset about these trifling things. I still think the word 'gay' has been cruelly misused, though."

*****

"Anyway, there's something else about the LGBT – or gay – community that bothers me. That's what I really wanted to talk to you about."

"Well, Clovis, what is it?"

"It's the way it has of drawing attention to itself. Oh, don't get me wrong, I'm not in the least bit homophobic, or against public demonstrations of single-sex behaviour, or gay priests, or gay marriages, or anything like that, but why must some LGBT people be so demonstrative about it? I mean, Gay Pride parades, alternative Gay World Cups, rainbow banners everywhere – for me, it's a little too much."

"Does it really matter? It doesn't do any harm, does it? And some people would say gay pride parades and such like, add a splash of colour to what otherwise can be a dull, and distinctly *un-gay* world, to revert to the original meaning of the term."

"In a general sense, no, it doesn't matter, and I agree that more colour in our lives is something we could all benefit from. But sometimes, quite often in fact, one has the feeling that LGBT activists have a single-minded mission to hijack all public awareness, whatever the cost, and to the detriment of other, equally if not more pressing causes...

"Take the recent World Cup in Qatar, for example. In the years, months and weeks leading up to the tournament, there was a good deal of protest about the awful treatment of Asian workers employed to build the stadiums and other infrastructure, about the environmental impact of huge, air-conditioned structures in the middle of the desert, <u>as well as</u> Qatar's caveman attitude towards gay people. But once the thing actually started – no more talk about the environment, or maltreatment of foreign workers – just gay rights, gay rights, and more gay rights. 'Should the England team be allowed to wear rainbow armbands?' Endless accounts of gay supporters being forced to conceal their sexual tendencies, and so on and so forth. All relevant, of course, but entirely eclipsing those other issues, which seemed to have disappeared completely from the public awareness."

"Maybe so, but that's not really the fault of the LGBT activists, is it? They're entitled to make their protests, and if other activists literally aren't as 'active' in promoting their own causes, that's not their problem after all?"

"Absolutely not – though I still think sometimes they go too far – in 'outing' public figures who aren't in fact gay, just to publicise their cause, for example. But what really bothers me – or puzzles me rather – is that, in our liberal-leaning part of the world at least where being gay is no longer seen as anything out of the ordinary, they seem to want to do everything <u>to make it seem</u> out of the ordinary. A very contradictory approach, in my humble opinion."

"I don't quite understand. What exactly do you mean, Clovis?"

"Well, if I were gay – which I'm not, of course – but if I were, I'd really want to simply be seen as just an ordinary individual. I wouldn't be secretive about it, but I wouldn't make a fuss about it. In a society that by and large no longer discriminates against me, I'd expect my sexuality to be accepted just as a part of my personality, nothing remarkable at all, just an unexceptional aspect of me. I'm sure that the large majority of gay men and women think exactly in this way."

"I'm sure they do."

"And so, if that's the case, I wouldn't think they can be all that happy to see all these flamboyant displays of gayness, which seem paradoxically to be saying 'look at me: I'm the same as you, but I'm different as well, and I want to display my different-ness by parading round in extravagant costumes, indulging in ultra-extrovert behaviour and reminding you that you shouldn't discriminate against me, even if you have no intention of doing so in the first place'."

"OK, I think I see what you mean."

"Well why are you sniggering away like that, then?"

"The first point you made was that the word 'gay' has been hijacked by the gay community. Now you seem to be condemning the gay community for being gay – that is, gay in the sense of bright, glittering, carefree, which is your preferred etymological meaning of the word."

"Oh, tush! You know <u>exactly</u> what I'm trying to get you to understand. I'm very gay myself, you know – in terms of my 'preferred etymological meaning of the word' as you put it – but I don't go around flaunting my gayness in any way at all. I'm really a very discreet, retiring individual."

"Well, Clovis, I'm not so sure about that..."

Conversation Number Four: Celebrity Normans

"Well now, Clovis, I don't suppose you've ever had much interest in parlour games, have you?"

"Parlour games? You mean, things like 'Charades', 'Hunt the Thimble', 'Squeak, Piggy Squeak'? No, not much interest in them – almost none at all, in fact. Oh, they can be fun at times I suppose, but quite undignified and rather rumbustious – some of them, at least."

"In general, I quite agree. One definitely has to be in the right mood. But sometimes they can help in killing time, when on a long car journey, for example. Not the rumbustious ones perhaps, but some of those that require a modicum of lateral thinking."

"Oh, I suppose so, if one is in the right mood, which usually one is not. Why do you ask? If you're thinking of a turn at 'I Spy' or something, really, I'm not very interested..."

"Actually no, don't worry, that's not it at all. I just want your opinion about something."

Clovis eyes me suspiciously. *"I think you already have the sum total of my opinion of parlour games. I suppose if one is a little drunk, they can have a certain appeal. I'm thinking of things like 'Cardinal Puff', for example, not that I've ever indulged in it myself, you understand."*

"Nothing to do with 'Cardinal Puff', or 'Fuzzy Duck', or 'Paranoia', or any of those other drinking games. What I want your opinion about is a _new_ parlour game I've invented, which happens to be called 'Celebrity Normans'."

"Well, as I'm sure you've noticed, these little amusements tend to have rather quirky names, so this one keeps up that tradition, at least. Anyway," yawning, *"tell me more, if you must."*

"Oh, it's completely silly, I know, but having tried it out a little people seem to respond well to it, especially when killing time, as I said before. It's quite good fun, and the rules are simple:

1. Person one must think of a name: 'Norman', 'Brian', 'Ronald', Dennis' - something like that.

2. Persons two, three, four etc. have exactly two minutes to think up as many celebrities they know who have the declared name. No cheating now! No

use of Google or Wikipedia! Come on, how many can you think of? Norman Wisdom, Norman Mailer, Stormin' Norman Schwartzkopf etc., etc... and yes, family names count too, so you can have Greg Norman the golfer, Barry Norman the TV presenter...

3. Sorry, time's up! What's that? What do you mean, 'can you include fictitious Normans?'. Well, no, they don't count, unless all competitors agree that they do... oh well, in that case, yes, I'll give you 'Spiny Norman' and Norman from 'Fireman Sam': but absolutely not females called Norma, so Norma Jeane Mortenson (aka Marilyn Monroe) definitely won't do!

4. The person who achieves the most Celebrity Normans then gets to choose the name for the next round – Celebrity Sandras, or Celebrity Simons, or whatever – and thus the game perpetuates itself.

So, Clovis, that's it in a nutshell: what do you think?"

Clovis (yawning again), *"Oh, not too bad, I suppose. Definitely an improvement on some of the others – the ones requiring silly, slightly risqué physical activities, in particular. Difficult to get more than mildly amused by it, however..."*

Kram Rednip: "Thanks, don't worry, I wasn't expecting you to be wildly enthusiastic: if you think it more or less passes muster, that's enough for me. It's just something I thought up for fun, after all it really is completely silly, isn't it?"

Clovis: "Yes, it is, but then silliness is an integral part of these things, isn't it? Anyway, now you've got it, what do you intend to do with it? Patent it? Franchise it to broadcasters across the world à la 'Who Wants to Make a Million' or whatever it's called?"

Kram: "No, nothing like that. Just offer it up as a mild form of amusement, when one is stuck in a group of people with nothing much to do. I've already done so a few times, as I've said, and it seems to go down quite well. The main problem for me with Celebrity Normans is that I've too long an experience with it to be able to compete fairly anymore. When I can't get to sleep at night, I play with myself (ahem!) thinking up as many Walters, Kevins, Lauras as I can muster. It doesn't generally help me get to sleep, but it does seem to make the *'nuit blanche'* pass more quickly…"

Clovis: "Well, that's something, I suppose. You can still be the question master, even if you can't participate. I'd take it rather badly if you tried to use the name 'Clovis', by the way, not that there are many Celebrity Clovises I can think of – apart from me, of course. The name "Kram" might prove something of a challenge, also. I'd steer clear of it, if I were you."

Chicken Kyiv

Olymipicky, Kyiv, January 2017

I've finally had to admit it. I'm chicken. I'm a coward, a Willie Wetlegs, a yellow-belly, no moral fibre or backbone at all. And it's taken me $61^{1/2}$ years of my life, and a cold winter in Kyiv, to realise this.

Winters in Kyiv, I was forewarned, are indeed *cold.* Ice, snow, grey skies, minus 20 temperatures, hardy fishermen being swept away on ice floes in the River Dnipro, lumps of ice falling off roofs onto pedestrians' heads; Ukrainians are, I think, rather proud of all this. My Ukrainian colleagues seem to take a grim pleasure in telling me how cold it's going to be next week. *'Oh yes, minus 25 during the night is forecast for tomorrow. But of course, this is normal for us. Some winters it is much worse than this…'* Otherwise, they are pretty stoical about it. They wrap up well, grumble a bit and just get on with things.

Well, I am pretty stoical about it too – in a general way. Even on the coldest workday mornings this last January, I have still enjoyed the little daily half-hour walk from apartment to office: out into the snow from the grubby front door of our apartment block, past the Metro and the synagogue, down into the underpass, along Kreshchatyk, before finally popping up - chilled but not stirred - into our office overlooked by the Art Museum. I too have learned to wrap up well, put on my stoutest Caterpillar boots and plenty of lip balm. But in one important respect I *can't* cope with it, and it is this that has caused me to finally acknowledge my inherent cowardliness.

It's the pavements. The malevolent pavements of Kyiv. In winter, they become slippery and treacherous, to the point that my daily half-hour walk (as above) quite frequently becomes a true ordeal. Or rather, a test in concentration - because one never knows exactly which bit of which pavement is going to catch one out. One spends all the time scrutinising the moving patch of - hopefully solid - ground on which one is about to place one's feet as one proceeds, crab-like, along the way. I use the word 'malevolent' because bits of pavement that one day are sound and firm underfoot for some reason become treacherous the next. Logically, I suppose this is the effect of more and more feet trampling on the same patch of snow or ice over successive days, allied to changes in climatic conditions – the amount of moisture in the air, whether there has been a light dusting of snow overnight, etc. But I really have come to believe that the Kyiv pavements have a vicious streak in them, that they are deliberately trying to get you to slip and fall over so they can have a good laugh about it. Maybe different stretches of pavement communicate with each other in some way as you walk along, so they know what to do when you are coming? Something like this….

"Hi, Kreshchatyk, it's the stairs down into the Metropad underpass here. Listen, you-know-who passed along here just five minutes ago, and he was looking particularly cagey this morning. Too late for us to send him arse-over-tip I'm afraid; we're totally clear today, but maybe you could arrange something? You know, some of those icy patches in front of the Dnipro Hotel, just slicken them up a bit and you could have a score. You could really send him flying. Hee! Hee! Hee!"

or:

"Basseyna calling. Look, you were completely dry yesterday, weren't you? Well, could you arrange a little slick this morning? Nothing too dramatic, just enough to instil a little false confidence in him as he walks along, so he steps out a bit too much, and then bang! Down he goes!"

****

Well, whether the paving stones do communicate with each other in this way or not, the upshot for me is the realisation that I am indeed... *Chicken Kyiv.*

How is it that the Ukrainians treat their treacherous underfoot conditions with so much disdain, compared with me? Every morning, as I scramble querulously along, I'm overtaken by dozens of *Kyivois* who don't seem to give a moment's thought that they might fall over. Some of them even show their contempt for the underfoot conditions by indulging in little impromptu skating sessions from time to time on suitably polished patches of ice. Me, on the other hand... I'm thoroughly terrified. I have all the forward momentum of a walrus, anxiously scrutinising each step ahead before planting my Caterpillar-booted right foot gingerly down while simultaneously worrying about where I'm going to next plant down the left one.

I've tried to rationalise things. *'I'm not used to it,'* I tell myself. *'These people have been dealing with this all their lives. They must have some technique or trick that keeps them perpendicular no matter how nonchalantly they stride along.'* Well, maybe there is something in this, but to all appearances they aren't walking any differently to me. I guess it's mostly a matter of confidence. You see quite a few women stepping out boldly in stilettos, even during the worst conditions - when the temperature rises a little, then it rains, then the rain freezes on contact and turns to ice, for example. Whenever this happens – I'm almost frozen (!) to the spot!

Or: *'I'm an old man, my knees aren't what they used to be. I just have to be careful.'* But this doesn't really wash, either – every day I'm shouldered out of the way by *babichkas* who, judging by the way they bustle along, must have a train to catch or something. They are older than me, less fit than me – but a lot braver than me! It's painful to admit but - after all, I must just be a confirmed, chicken-livered coward.

****

It snowed heavily the other night, so my daily progress was even more crab or walrus-like than usual. On my way, I encountered one of the phenomena of winter in Kyiv – the man who drives the snowplough along the pavements of Kreshchatyk. This man's main ambition in life seems to be to sweep aside the pedestrians, as well as the snow. He roars along at 90 mph, swerving around alarmingly and forcing those in his path to jump aside smartly if they don't want to end up half-buried in the metre-high trail of virgin snow that marks his passage, either side of the walkway. Maybe there's a Formula One competition for snowplough drivers…

How I'd love to be him! No fear of falling over, no slipping and sliding, just a powerful motor and a wide set of caterpillar tracks to swoosh around on. Maybe he has a malevolent streak. Maybe he's a coward, just like me.

Sex on the Internet

Those of you to have persevered this far in reading these stories will have noticed my *penchant* for catchy titles. Well, they don't come much catchier, or more lurid, than this! But as you've probably come to expect with catchy titles in our grab-your-attention-at-any-price modern age, the content of what follows is usually disappointingly un-lurid in comparison with the titivation quotient up-front.

In fact, really not wanting to promise more than I could deliver, I almost called this piece *'Genari Karganoff'*. Either title would have been perfectly legitimate, since in it I'm going to cover both subjects: sex, that is, and the obscure late 19th century Russian composer of that name. Quite a contrast! *'What could the link between them possibly be?'* I hear you ask. Well, as you'll soon see, it's my adventures with the internet. How to explain? I think I'm going to begin with Genari Karganoff!

****

Genari Karganoff is a composer so obscure that he doesn't even feature in my fairly comprehensive reference book, *'The Lives of the Great Composers'* by Harold C. Schonberg.

I first came across him years and years ago, when as a boy in Sheffield I was learning the piano and studying for the Royal Schools of Music exams. One of the pieces I had to learn for the Grade IV (Intermediate) level in 1971 was a lively little scherzo of his. I must have played it quite well in the exam, since I achieved a 'merit' rating overall, with a score of 123 points out of 150; the Karganoff would have been a major element in this.

This was at the period in my life when I was, effectively, being forced to learn to play the piano by my parents. For my mother it was a 'genteel' thing to do, while my father, from time to time, quoted at me the tale of a cousin of his who had risen to become managing director of Firth Brown - the biggest steel producer in Sheffield - on account of his prowess at the keyboard having been noticed by the Powers That Be (or That Then Were). A little fanciful of my father, perhaps. Anyway, I was quite talented as a junior pianist, but being cowed into it in the way I was, I didn't enjoy it at all.

I almost dropped the piano altogether as I progressed through my teens, only discovering a real interest in playing later in adult life. However, having kept many of my old folios of examination music, as an adult I hunted them out and started playing some of the pieces again. The Karganoff scherzo is not particularly difficult technically, but it has some charm and requires a certain level of dexterity to play properly; so I amused myself in working it up again. Then one day, while rummaging through a dusty old box of sheet music, in some second-hand bookshop, in some Eastern European capital where I happened to be working, (Zagreb, I think it was) I came across a venerable but well-preserved edition of the suite of which the piece formed a part: Opus 21, *'Album for the Young'*.

So many composers have produced anthologies of children's pieces, usually easy enough to play, but frequently containing a freshness and vigour less evident in their more 'serious' compositions. I therefore addressed Karganoff's little anthology with enthusiasm, and soon became competent at various other delightful little works: *'A la Hongroise'*, *'Dance of the Elves'*, *'Polka'*, and a few others. And as for me, the Music is the Man, I then turned to the to try and discover something about Genari Karganoff, life and times.

In general, I've found the internet very useful indeed in extending my knowledge of the more minor composers that I've become interested in. For example, I've discovered that Franz Kuhlau lost an eye at an early age, which indirectly led him - while convalescing - to become a musician. I've learnt that Dussek was a fine concert pianist and was known as 'the handsome'. I've discovered that the Irish composer John Field, who spent most of his working life in St Petersburg, is generally credited as being the originator of that Chopinesque musical form, the nocturne. But with Karganoff, I drew an almost complete blank. In fact, even worse than a blank, because the few websites I found that could tell me anything at all about him, offered up highly contradictory information. Was his name Karganoff, Karganov or Korganov? Was he Russian or Georgian? Was *'Album for the Young'* his opus 21 or 25? Most sites with a reference to him, had him being born in 1858 and dying in 1890, but one or two had him lingering on well into the 20th century; where was the real truth about this man? Wikipedia - my usual first port of call in my researches - was completely silent on him, and wildly off-beam: when I typed in his name, the best it could come up with was 'Jenn-Air Products'.

So I ended up, frustratingly, not much more the wiser about him; the inconsistencies in what I unearthed being particularly frustrating. But then, when you think about it, *how reliable is the internet* as a source of information? Pretty reliable perhaps in a general sense, but prone to lapses of accuracy or logic, that I suppose reflects no more than the unedited nature of the research done by the people who create the entries. Consider, for example, my little conundrum concerning ess, ee, ex…

****

'On average, men have 9 different sexual partners during their lives, while for women the average is 7.25'.

This little titbit is something I picked up on 'Yahoo!' one day recently. It was the outcome of a 'comprehensive survey into modern sexual practices', and supposedly based on extensive research. It made me feel rather small, of course, because for every inadequate male in the world like me, there must be some rampant, red-blooded Rambo with a tally of 15-20 or more 'scores', just to keep the masculine average up to par.

But hang on a minute! I have a problem with the logic of these survey findings: how can the number of sexual partners for men and women respectively differ? Are they taking the number as an average over the total population in the world, or for any specific group? Isn't it logically obvious that – as an average – the number must be identical (or almost so, at least) for both sexes?

OK, in stating this, I'm assuming two things: first, that the number of men and women in the population is roughly the same, and that there are roughly the same number of heterosexuals among both. But otherwise, I propose a little experiment of my own to demonstrate the validity of my assertion...

The Desert Island Hypothesis

On a desert island there are five men and five women.
Man no. 1 has sex with all five women.
Man no. 2 has sex with woman no.1 and woman no.2.
Man no.3 has no sex at all.
Man no.4 has sex with women nos. 1, 3 and 5.
Man no.5 has sex with woman no. 5 only.

Therefore, the five men have a total of 11 sexual partners, being an average of 2.2 per man.

This means that:

Woman no. 1 has sex with men nos.1, 2 and 4.
Woman no. 2 has sex with man no.1 and man no.2.
Woman no. 3 has sex with man no.1 and man no. 4.
Woman no. 4 has sex with man no.1.
Woman no. 5 has sex with men nos.1, 4 and 5.

Therefore, the five women have a total of 11 sexual partners, being an average of 2.2 per woman.

You see? It's logically (and to my mind obviously) impossible that the men can have more sexual partners than the women, because every male sexual partner automatically means an equivalent female sexual partner.

So, the survey published on Yahoo! Tells me two things:

First of all, men are liars regarding their sexual prowess. There is nothing very surprising in this, I suppose. What would be interesting to know, however, is whether women are liars as well? Do women understate the number of sexual partners they have? (in which case the real average would be somewhere between 7.25 and 9) or do they too exaggerate (in which case the real average is probably something less than 7.25)? Impossible, I suppose, to ever really know the truth. Perhaps I should ask my wife what she thinks?

Secondly, the internet is a highly unreliable source of information. The fact that so obvious a false statistic can be paraded by a reputable website such as Yahoo! tells me so. More than a little surprising is that those responsible for creating Yahoo!'s web pages could be so slipshod. However…

Anyway, if they can make mistakes, so can I – deliberately. I have it in mind to prepare my own 'Wikipedia' entry for Genari Karganoff; calling on my imagination to make up the deficit of verifiable information about the man, I might indulge in something like this:

'Jennairi Karganoff (or Karganzdorff) was a Bulgarian composer who died in 1990 at the age of 132. He ascribed his longevity to his vigorous sex life, once calculating that he had an average of 9 lovers for every year of his life,

making a total of 1,188 sexual partners during his whole lifetime. His monumental seminal work 'Album for the Young' (opus 29) is regarded as one of the finest examples of late 19th-century romantic composition...'

Thus, my unique contribution to the great body of knowledge on the internet!

Terry's Tale: Basic Animal Instincts

A story of contemporary office life

The team of consultants were all sitting in White Shop, Georgetown, Guyana, drinking rum, beer and finishing off their plates of fish and chips.

Terry guffawed suddenly. "I could tell you a funny story about that."

"About what? Basic animal instincts? The law of the jungle? Not one of your tales about Uganda, by any chance?"

"No, nothing at all to do with Uganda, and I'm sorry, James, if my stories bore you. Do you remember Mickey Marlbury?"

"Not really, no, name rings a bell. Wasn't he a consultant in Salzburg's group?"

"Yeah, that's right, he was, but he was shafted about a year ago. You know why he was shafted?"

"No, of course not."

"Well, that's the funny story. That's what I'm going to tell you about."

Terry chortled to himself again, stubbed out his latest cigarette and took a pull at his beer bottle. His story went like this.

"As you've not been to the new London offices yet, you

won't know what they're like: a typical 1980s block, all smoked glass and marble finishing, on six floors overlooking the Old Bailey. All floors are open-plan apart from the partner's offices, and even most of those are only little glass cubicles stuck in the corners on each floor. Well, open-plan's a fair enough policy as long as there's enough space for everyone; everyone has somewhere to sit, you can walk around and talk to people, and you don't feel there's someone looking over your shoulder all the time. But problems begin when things start to get overcrowded. Then tensions start to creep in, tempers get frayed, and people's territorial instincts start to take over. That's more or less what happened to Mickey Marlbury, only with him he took it to extremes.

"Business was still good two or three years back, so of course the firm was taking on new hires all the time. Only way to grow the business, the partners were always telling us. Well, you can't fit a quart into a pint pot and pretty soon the situation was that they implemented a 'hot desking' policy. You know what I mean by that? It's simple, really: nobody has their own desk or workspace, they just install workstations with computers and everything else you need, and you simply come into the building, find a free space and get on with your work. In theory it doesn't matter that there are more people than workstations, the logic goes that most people are going to be out at clients at least 50 percent of the time, so there should always be somewhere available to sit and get on with your work.

"That's the theory, and I must say that most of the time it works well enough in practice, too. There may have been a couple of occasions, when I was working in London, when I had to wander around the building for some time trying to find somewhere to sit, but usually, in the end, you could find somewhere, even if it wasn't thoroughly suitable. But the problem with hot desking is simple: people don't like it. It's disruptive, downright unnerving in fact, when you don't know where you're going to be, who you'll be sitting next to, or even where the nearest loos and coffee machines are. It cuts across the most basic office mentality instinct of all, the need for your own little space which you make your own in the midst of all the impersonality.

"Well, pretty soon, people started finding their own ways to disrupt the hot desking policy. What most of them did, in fact, was simple enough: if they couldn't have their own actual work area, they'd jolly well create one and make sure that no-one else encroached on it. Just basic, territorial instincts in fact. What most people did was personalise their own little corner: you know, have framed pictures of their families on the desk, pin up postcards, cartoons, funny slogans, things like that. Usually it worked: everyone understood that such and such desk was so and so's corner, and that even if it was vacant, you weren't to sit there unless there really was nowhere else to go.

"Mickey Marlbury: well, he was territorial even before the open desk policy came into being. He was a clever guy, quite a nice guy in some ways - but idiosyncratic. I knew him quite well, as I was a manager in Salzburg's group a few years ago, when he was taken on. Frankly, he rubbed quite a few people up the wrong way. I don't know why, exactly. I suppose he had his own ideas about things and didn't hesitate to tell other people what they were. The little things he did, it was as if he was always deliberately trying to be different from all the rest of us. For example, he wouldn't drink tea and coffee from the machine: he had his own teapot which he brewed up regularly on his desk, even his own milk and sugar bowl. I remember he had a wooden effigy on his desk as well - one of those things with detachable arms, legs and feet that you can manipulate into different postures and so on. Charlie Snell - another guy in the group who was recruited about the same time as Mickey - hated all Mickey's little ways, and made a point of letting him know about it. I remember once, he removed the head off the wooden effigy and buried it in the sugar bowl. Mickey didn't find it for weeks afterwards.

"Mickey was quite a good consultant and I think he might have survived, despite his strange little ways, if it hadn't been for the hot desking policy. At first, it didn't matter too much as there were enough other places around the building for squatters to move into. Nobody moved into his space just because it was so obviously personalised, with his teapot, his wooden effigy, and a whole load of other things besides. But pretty quickly the staff numbers grew, and there must have been a slack period when a lot of people were hanging around in the office, and didn't have clients to go to, and eventually someone took the plunge. I wasn't in the office myself at the time, but I heard all about it. It was one of the newly recruited graduates from one of the other groups, who didn't know Mickey, and didn't remember a time before hot desking, and probably didn't even think twice about what he was doing. After all, why should he? From what I heard, Mickey turned up mid-afternoon to find this guy had cleared away all his paraphernalia from his desk, and was sitting there doing some work as if it was his own. Well, he just did his nut. You know, shouting, and swearing, I don't know if he actually tried to punch the poor guy but apparently there was some kind of a scuffle, and it took all the other consultants quite a while to sort things out between them. They tried to hush it up, but of course old Salzburg got to hear about it, and he gave poor Mickey a complete dressing-down. Told him to clear away all his stuff from his workspace, and that he was lucky the firm didn't do him for assault.

"Well, Mickey did clear away most of his stuff, but he obviously wasn't happy about it. The worst of it was, as word got round about what had happened, he got shunned by a lot of the managers who would otherwise have given him client work, so he was stuck in the office even more than he had been previously. It was a vicious, downwards spiral that he couldn't escape from. So basically, what he did was find another workstation as far away from the partner offices as possible, and just sat there and sulked. After some time, most of his artefacts put in an appearance again, so there he was, just the same as before. Of course, nobody dared to try and disturb him. We all just left him alone, in his little private world in the corner.

"I don't know exactly what happened after that, several different versions of the story went round after Mickey was given the push. What is certain is that he started behaving very, very strangely. It was said that the first signs of odd behaviour were the noises he started making: clicking his tongue, whistling, breaking wind loudly, and so forth. Most people were too embarrassed to go near him, or investigate further. Then someone apparently caught him urinating on the carpet around his workstation - you know, as if he was trying to lay down a scent to warn off other male consultants not to come near. He certainly succeeded, if that <u>was</u> his aim! How long things would have gone on without anybody doing anything I don't know, but the story goes that one afternoon Mickey grabbed hold of one of the female consultants and tried to drag her back into his corner. That was the end, of course. He was marched out of the building, together with all his personal property, and never allowed near the place again. The partners aren't completely heartless, though; they stopped short of doing him for sexual harassment at work."

Terry chuckled and drained off the last of his rum and water. "So it just goes to show, in my opinion anyway, that we haven't moved upwards all that far from the animals. It doesn't take much for our basic animal instincts to come bubbling up to the surface: at least, in poor old Mickey's case, it didn't."

James leaned back in his chair, and grinned.

"I heard something about that story as well, though I'm not sure you haven't exaggerated a bit about the urinating and all that. But you're dead right about animal instincts. I don't know if young Kram here would agree with us. It looks as if his instinct right now is to get some sleep."

We Need to Talk about C***D

Village de Massigne, France, 2021

It's been a long time since I've put together one of my little stories. Frankly, for a long time I couldn't think of anything to write about. Being a self-disciplined sort of chap, I did try for a while after my last successful effort - 'Chicken Kyiv', I think it was – but all my half-hearted attempts petered out in apathy and failure. Eventually I just gave up and channelled my intellectual gymnastics into my piano-playing instead.

And then - quite suddenly, a couple of days ago - and idea came to me about a subject I feel I might develop into something. Paradoxically, it isn't at all original. In fact, it's a subject that, after almost two years, I've become sick and tired of hearing people bang on about. Can you guess what it is? Of *course* you can, it's COVID!!!

Not so much paradoxical as hypocritical of me to write about it. I'm always saying, to family members and others, that I'm fed up with hearing about it. For months and months now, it has just dominated all human interaction completely. No matter what kind of gathering – family party, or a get-together among friends, or even chance meetings with total strangers – sooner or later everyone starts talking about it. Everyone has an opinion, and everyone wants to let everyone else know what that opinion is. It's just so depressing. Don't get me wrong, I know the great pandemic is a very serious matter, that we all have responsibilities relating to it and that we all want to see the back of it. But still, if only it could be *talked* into oblivion, we'd already be well on our way to being rid of it.

***

First of all, I have a confession to make. I have *not* been vaccinated, and all things being equal I don't intend to be. Shock! Horror! What an antisocial beast you are, Kram Rednip! Well… maybe. I don't consider myself an 'Anti-Vaxxer', and I certainly don't believe all the stuff that circulates on the internet about vaccine health hazards, vaccine conspiracy theories etc. I simply consider that a) I have a strong immune system that I don't want messed about with, b) now that I'm retired, I have limited social contact anyway, and c) I'm very careful in wearing a mask and sticking to social distancing guidelines. But of course, this is not enough for the self-righteous vaccinated, or indeed for many politicians.

In particular, for His Excellency (or His Majesty?) the President of France, who, in ramping up restrictions on the unvaccinated like me, has threatened menacingly to *enmerde* me (a slang expression generally translated into English as 'to piss someone off': I would put it rather as 'to bugger things up for someone'). Actually, despite the imminent appearance of the famous *passe vaccinale,* in the short term nothing much changes for me as already I can't go to the cinema, swimming pool, restaurant etc. and am resigned to a life as a sort of Covid-related leper. I don't mind all that much, but I *am* concerned, in view of M. Macron's sentiments, that the restrictions will probably become more severe, *or even that the anti-vaccination rhetoric at government level could stir up some kind of violent response at street level, perhaps even the formation*

*of 'Anti-Anti-Vax Vigilante Groups' marauding about with
the mission of harassing or attacking the non-vaccinated –
like me.* Who knows? Could things descend towards a
Covid-related equivalent of *Kristallnacht*, perhaps?

All this is quite scary, and although I know one is not
supposed to compare the treatment of the unvaccinated with
the treatment of the Jews in Germany in the 1930s (an
Austrian politician was roundly criticised recently for doing
just this), the possibility of more severe recrimination does
make me feel slightly uncomfortable.

***

This leads me on to the main point I wish to make.

Never, during my whole life to date, can I claim that I have
been a member of a minority that has been subject to
discrimination. I am white, I am not homosexual, I am not
of a racial or cultural group shunned by the majority or
treated as suspect (think of Travelling People or
'Manouches' as they are pejoratively called in France) nor
am I a Catholic (would have been subject to severe
discrimination had I lived in 16th-century England). Thus, I
have gone through my life to date without knowing what it
is to be ostracised – or persecuted. However, that is no
longer the case. I am subject to the creeping, gradual process
of *enmerdisation* by the French government – maybe soon
to be denied access to shopping centres, and even hospitals
– and also to the sideways glances and sometimes openly
snide remarks of people I meet who know already or come
to discover that I am not fulfilling my civic duty apropos
COVID to the standards they expect.

Of course, what I currently undergo, and even what I am likely to be subject to in future, assuming that measures to limit the freedoms of the unvaccinated are increased by way of 'gentle persuasion' can only be described as a very mild form of discrimination, and nothing at all to compare with the suffering of so many minorities both currently and throughout history. Nevertheless, being in this position gives me a funny feeling. On one hand - being rather stubborn, perhaps – it makes me want to continue my resistance, perhaps just because I resent being pressured into doing something I don't want to do. On the other, it makes me realise to some degree, and for the first time in my life, what it actually is to be considered undesirable and subject to recrimination and punishment *just because* one is different from the majority. A position millions of people throughout the world are in, with no possibility of doing anything about it. Accordingly, I have an increased sense of respect for 'Black Lives Matter' and other similar movements; and, I hope, a better understanding of what being discriminated against feels like.

***

'Discrimination versus persecution': is there a fixed line between them? I suppose not - it rather depends on one's personal circumstances. For example, I've already strongly indicated that what I suffer from being unvaccinated amounts to discrimination, and no more. But what if I were working, and was fired from my job for failing to get jabbed? This has, of course, actually happened to many health workers and others. Little doubt in my mind that in such cases the line has been crossed, that many people in

France and elsewhere have been deprived of their source of income or significant liberties as a result of their decision not to conform. And where will it end if the great pandemic continues to throw up bad surprises (aka variants) that prolong the crisis for months or even years to come?

I suppose it could end in compulsory vaccination for all. Personally, I would probably reluctantly go along with this, and step back over the threshold of conformity and civic obedience – like a 16th-century Catholic agreeing to renounce his or her faith just to avoid continued harassment. As for those who continue to resist – well, they should be burned at the stake, shouldn't they?

Kulture Shock – Part One: TV Commercials

How do you identify the real culture and identity of a nation?

I've found the answer. It's very simple. All you have to do is watch television.

Or – more specifically, the commercials aired on television. They tell you immediately all you need to know about the values and attitudes of the local populace.

This was brought home to me recently while watching a cricket match on TV (The West Indies v. England) in Trinidad. Cricket matches must be an advertiser's dream, because at the end of each six-ball over there is a sufficient break for the airing of at least one commercial before the next over begins. There are also less frequent but longer drinks breaks of about five minutes, enabling several commercials to be shown. It was during a drinks break (very welcome: the West Indies had England on the ropes, 39 for 5 in their second innings) that my Eureka Moment occurred. There were four successive commercials – for White Oak Rum, Carib Beer, Kentucky Fried Chicken and a brand of potato crisps the name of which I can't remember – *and all of them were exactly the same.* They all featured a group of healthy, attractive, smiling young people - on the beach, in a bar, jigging about, having a party – while collectively enjoying the product being offered. Honestly, you could have juxtaposed any of the products being promoted with any of the commercials, and you wouldn't have seen any difference or glaring incongruity.

It really would be hard to devise a more accurate

presentation of the Caribbean attitude to life than that presented in this series of commercials. As a Trini explained to me when I described my experience to her, 'Here in the Caribbean, work is seen just as an unfortunately necessary interval between the 'liming'*'. Hmm: I guess this explains a lot about the project I'm currently engaged in in Port of Spain, which has encountered a succession of delays throughout its progress due to breaks in the working routine (Christmas and New Year; Carnival, Easter, upcoming elections, Eid, Diwali, etc.).

This made me reflect on the fact that TV commercials are very different in other parts of the world, but are equally reflective of the national values of the nation in which they happen to be aired. For example:

- In France, the main focus is on food products, as one might expect - and family cars. Lots of classy commercials presenting the latest Renault X, or Peugeot Y, usually involving cool, floppy-haired young people enjoying a drive through dramatic rocky countryside or modernistic cityscapes.

- In the UK by contrast, there is a strong focus on the household and domestic products. Cleaning products, DIY products, cookery aids; immediately

*See 'Trinidad Confidential'; in accord with my old friend, Clovis Buckram, I do wonder sometimes about the Trinidadian attitude to having fun. It seems to me they consider it almost an obligation – you must enjoy yourself, even if you're not, very much. Some of the festivities around Carnival – being crammed together in a crowd, watching noisy and repetitive pan music while slowly getting drunk, for example – come into this category. But maybe I'm just being an old fart in agreeing with Clovis on this….

after Christmas, a curious explosion of ads for three-piece suites, mattresses and the like. *'Come to Snoozoland where for the whole of January we're having our HALF PRICE SALE!'*

- And then, there are the commercials coming from the USA. Many of these I am also privileged to watch during my sojourns in the Caribbean, since so many downmarket US TV channels pop up there on satellite TV.

American TV Commercials; an apologia...

These I now regard as a kind of entertainment sideshow in themselves, rather than an exasperatingly-too-frequent interruption to whatever show I happen to be watching. They are just *so* cheesy, so revelatory of those aspects of the American psyche that I find bemusing; the laboured, jokey scenarios, the relentless bonhomie, the obsession with personal appearance, sexual performance and health issues. Above all, those ridiculous disclaimers by the sellers of healthcare products ('Don't take Doomadrene if you suffer from high blood pressure, piles, are pregnant or suffering from a slight cold...') presumably inserted to avoid any possibility of legal action from clients. In some cases, the disclaimers take up more than 50% of the whole airtime of the commercial. Doesn't this just scare any potential consumers off? Do people *actually buy* any of these products after viewing them?

Well, I assume they do, or the commercials wouldn't be aired with such relentless regularity. There is one particularly long one that pops up on ESPN for acne treatment, which is unvaryingly repeated *twice* during *every* half-time interval of *all* football matches being broadcast. I know the screenplay off by heart now... *'And now I have clear skin! I never thought my skin could look so good!'* Perhaps the repetition is the trick, is it just the constant relaying of an identical message that eventually gets through the viewer's defences? Or perhaps it's the inherent scare-factor relating to erectile dysfunction, or constipation, or just simply not having white teeth and a confident, wholesome appearance. Many of the ailments or personal inadequacies described in these TV commercials are so obscure: Pseudobulbar Affect (PBA) for example, apparently characterised by uncontrollable crying or laughing. Before I saw a commercial promoting a treatment for it, I'd never heard of it, or of anyone suffering from it. Which leads me to ask myself the question: *does it actually exist?* Is there really such an ailment, or has it just been invented by a drugs company in order to scare credible and over-emotional but otherwise healthy people into believing they actually have a health problem, and need only to buy their product in order to recover? How easy this would be – why, I think I'll have a go myself!

Hyperventilated Earlobe Syndrome (HES)

Scene: a pensive-looking, middle-aged lady is pruning roses in the garden. Relaxing background music is softly playing in a minor key.

Pensive middle-aged lady ('Cindy'): *'The first thing I noticed was a slight twitching of my earlobes. I thought*

---

nothing of it for a while… but then the twitching and tingling became much stronger and persistent, I realised my earlobes were turning slightly more pink, sometimes even feeling a bit painful…''

Voice-over (in a concerned, sympathetic tone of voice): *Many people in America suffer from Hyperventilated Earlobe Syndrome, or HES. When they don't take it seriously, it can lead to persistent irritation and embarrassment and sometimes, as in Cindy's case, actual physical pain…*

Cindy: '*… it got so bad that in the end I was just too embarrassed to go out anymore. I couldn't face my family and my friends. I was depressed, anxious, irritable… I lost my job, I even thought about taking my own life. I was living an absolute nightmare, I mean, how could folks take me seriously when my earlobes were turning slightly more pink?'*

V-O (sounding even more concerned): *Cindy's feelings are only too common in people who suffer from HES. It's a condition that can quickly turn your whole day into a living nightmare, with no way out and no-one to help you cope with the mental discomfort and the embarrassment that never goes away.*

Cut to Cindy looking anxious. The background music has developed a threatening edge, and dark clouds are now looming over the rose garden.

V-O: *But now there is a way out - with Lobodrene V Plus!*

Cut to Cindy looking happy again. Sunshine has been restored to the rose garden.

V-O: *Lobodrene V Plus strikes at the heart of HES by directly reducing that concentration of unsightly red blood corpuscles in and around your earlobes that is the cause of HES. Yes, just one capsule taken every day can scatter those corpuscles leading to alleviation of the symptoms within just a few weeks! Lobodrene V Plus is a simple, painless and perfectly natural remedy that can transform your life and restore you to full happiness – instantly. So why wait? Try Lobodrene V Plus today and the roses in your garden will never smell sweeter...*

Cut to Cindy looking beautiful and serene with her bunch of roses. She is smiling blandly and her eyes sparkle with gratitude and joy.

Cindy: '*Oh thank you, thank you, you folks at Lobodrene V Plus! You've given me my life back again! I just can't tell you how much Lobodrene V Plus has transformed my life!!*'

Earnest second voice-over (speaking breathlessly, hurriedly, seriously:

Don'ttakeLobodreneVPlusifyousufferfromshortnessofb
reathorheartburnorifyoufeeldizzyaftercleaningyourteet
hdon'ttakeLobodreneVPlusrifyourdoctoradvisesyoutoc
utdownondrivingyourcaronmajorroadsordrinkingteawi
thmilkandsugarinitdon'ttakeLobodreneVPlusafterwatc
hingrealityTVprogrammesandincaseswhereyourwifeis
Mexicanalwaysfollowyourdoctor'sadviceandneveruseL
obodreneVPlusforrecreationaldrugpurposes…

Maybe this is how they do it!!! It's so easy….

Step 1: dream up an ailment. Not something seriously life-threatening perhaps, but something close to the American psyche: mildly disfiguring, or limiting one's ability to lead a full lifestyle ('did you know that 90% of men over 40 suffer from some form of erectile dysfunction…?').

Step 2: manufacture a product to relieve the 'ailment'. As long as the ingredients are not actually life-threatening (and even if they are you have the disclaimer to fall back on if anyone actually dies after taking it) it should probably contain a mix of sedatives or anti-depressants or other substances that, once taken, are likely to make takers feel better about themselves.

Step 3: produce and broadcast a commercial promoting said product. Make sure to emphasise that the 'ailment' is quite normal and widespread, but can easily be cured (cut to 'special offer' mode): *'Lobodrene V Plus is available from main street pharmacies at 150 dollars for a month's supply. But we're offering not one, not two, but THREE months' supply for 50 DOLLARS!! Yes, that's right, just 50 DOLLARS! So why wait? This offer is for a limited period only, so call today on 0800 800 800 'Lobodrene' and we'll deliver within three days....'*

I enjoyed writing that… of course I'm being fanciful, as usual, but possibly only slightly so. Take PBA, for example. I accept it's a condition that <u>does</u> exist, the drugs company hasn't invented it, but what they've probably done is raise the 'scare factor' in their commercial so that emotionally vulnerable or hypochondriac viewers are stampeded into buying their product. After all, the major drugs companies, American and otherwise, do little to reduce the impression that they are pretty much totally immoral; using their patents and financial clout to block attempts to produce cheaper alternatives of their drugs, for Third World use, for example, or testing highly dangerous new products on impecunious 'human guinea pigs'. So I wouldn't entirely put it past them to completely invent a medical condition, just to boost their already ginormous profits.

****

Back to the telly in Trinidad. Inevitably, the West Indies won the cricket Test Match, by five wickets. Long before the end I'd switched over to one of the few commercial-free TV channels available via my satellite dish – Encore Westerns.

Kulture Shock – Part Two: Encore Westerns

I've always enjoyed watching westerns. I don't really know why, although I think it probably goes back to my boyhood in Lusaka in the early 1960s when – with no access to television – a regular source of entertainment was going with my parents to see films at the 'drive-in' cinema on the outskirts of town. In that era, the western was probably the most popular cinematographic 'genre' going, so I suppose it's quite natural that an impressionable little boy like me became an addict…

'This was the period when westerns were very much in vogue, and I presume my lifelong fascination with westerns comes from evenings spent at the drive-in, watching what, in many cases, were probably B-films with strongly stereotyped ethical values and storylines. For me, even now, the cornier a western is the more I like it. My big idol when I was a small boy was John Wayne, who for me epitomised everything that was brave and manly in a screen hero.'

The fascination has always stuck, so my discovery of the American TV channel 'Encore Westerns' has led to many happy hours slobbing out in front of the screen in my rented Port of Spain apartment. Encore Westerns 'does what it says on the tin' – it broadcasts nothing but westerns. In addition to films there are lots and lots of TV western-series episodes from the late '50s and early '60s (missed as a boy due to lack of TV coverage as mentioned above) which I can now devour greedily – 'Gunsmoke', 'Cheyenne', 'The Legend of Wyatt Earp', and 'Wanted Dead or Alive' starring a young Steve McQueen; some of them with surprisingly original storylines adding spice to the standard ingredients of the genre: the square-jawed, high-moral-fibre hero, the bristle-jawed bad guy, the saloon brawl, the shoot-out on the main street, the woman who stands by her man, etc.

I take my westerns seriously, I don't like the kind of 'jokey' westerns which sometimes appear, so when a 1970s episode of 'Death Valley Days' appeared on the TV, I immediately started surfing the channels in search of something else more suited to my tastes in entertainment. A pretty unproductive trawl it turned out to be – no football or cricket, no watchable films, lots of American network channels of absolutely no interest at all, in the end I settled in desperation on 'Pawn Stars' on 'The History Channel' – pretty lowbrow stuff, often irritating, but some form of mild amusement at least.

'Often irritating': I used to get much more uptight about American quasidocumentary and reality TV programmes than I do now. Isn't it generally said that the older one gets, the more intolerant one gets, as old age sets in one morphs gradually into grumpy-old-man- (or woman-) hood? Well, with me, the opposite seems to be the case, the older I become the more tolerant I become. I'm now much more laid back about things and people I used to loathe – aggressive drivers, Birmingham accents, the Olympic Games, even Tony Blair… and, pertinently to 'Pawn Stars', American TV commercials, as described in Part 1. Just as well, the commercial breaks are so frequent that you get about 50% commercial to 50% programme. 'Pawn Stars' maybe lowbrow, but it's quite compelling viewing for someone like me who appreciates antiques, and the quirky personalities of the 'stars' themselves, though hugely stereotyped, are fun to follow…

The History Channel, National Geographic Channel - franchises that pop up pretty regularly on the satellite menus one comes across in hotels in remote countries, Burundi for instance – where I worked recently. NGC is owned by that iconic US institution, National Geographic – as is its associated channel, 'Nat Geo Wild' – which focuses exclusively on wildlife topics, most of which seem to involve shaggy-haired, tough-guy characters, usually redneck Americans or Australians, wrestling with alligators and crocodiles for one reason or another.

But *are* National Geographic/Nat Geo Wild the TV channels owned by National Geographic, the publisher? I started to have doubts recently, in view of the fact that the stiffly erudite style of the monthly magazines produced by N.G. the publisher is so different from the dumbed-down stuff that frequently appears on the TV channels. So I referred to the internet to discover that yes, indeed N.G. got into commercial difficulties a few years ago, so sold the rights on its TV franchise to the notoriously downmarket Newsgroup (Murdoch) Corporation. This is the worldwide institution that serves up 'Sky News' etc., publishes 'The Sun' in the UK, and until the recent scandals concerning its dark journalistic practices (phone-tapping, etc.) also published 'The News of The World'… this discovery told me a lot about why Nat Geo programmes are what they frequently are.

So – I hear you ask – what kind of a problem do I have with Nat Geo? Many of its broadcasts are quite entertaining, after all (especially over a wet weekend in Bujumbura or Port of Spain, when there's bugger all else to do than stay in one's hotel room and watch TV). Well, let me give you some examples of the sort of stuff I've been subjected to…

Mudcats

This bafflingly ridiculous broadcast reflects as well as any the fact that National Geographic Channel exists essentially to serve an American audience - and a redneck hillbilly American audience at that. The format involves several two-man teams of fishermen (mostly looking like members of a Bikers' Chapter – tattooed, blobbily overweight, moustachioed and bandana-bound) who leap out of speedboats into shallow, murky stretches of river and wrestle sizeable catfish back into the boats with their bare hands. They then race off to the mustering point to weigh their captures, the team with the biggest fish winning a rather modest cash prize. Lots of whooping and stereotypically redneck bravado accompanies all of this:

'Whoo-hoop! Sure, Cat-daddy used to be the best, but this year I'm gonna whoop his ass…'

'It's gettin' reeel personal between me an' that ol' mudcat. Only one of us is gonna win this thing, and that's gonna be me. I guess he reckons he's got me beat, but I ain't finished with him yet, not by a long way, NOOOO man. I'm a'goin' back to his hole an' I'm a'gonna finish this thing the way it's gotta be finished…'

Mudcat wrestling is presented as a highly dangerous activity, but clearly it isn't; the worst that ever seems to happen to any of the fisherman is that he gets his fingers bitten by one of the poor, ugly, frightened beasts he's been dragging out of its hidey-hole. It's just crass, messy, pointless and environmentally deplorable. Shame on you, National Geographic Channel, for serving up such stuff!

Dog Whisperer

A diminutive Mexican-American who conducts endless dog training. The dogs are invariably basket cases with extreme inter-doggy social problems, but all are brought swiftly to heel (literally) by the calm, composed manner of said Mexican American. He is then effusively thanked by dog owner and moves on to the next basket case. Repetitively predictable, as soon as I see him coming, I switch over to watch something more interesting on another freebie channel; Australian rugby league, commercials for labour-saving household appliances, whatever.

'The 1980s'

Nostalgia rules! This was a highly publicised in advance series of 'special' programmes, each presenting a different aspect of the decade: fashion, music, innovation, etcetera – yet again from a strictly US of A perspective. Lots of interviews with ageing, long-forgotten celebrities, lots of slightly faded, slightly grainy 1980s footage of people with strange hairdos and enormous spectacles, *lots and lots* of use of the word 'awesome' (a term that seems to have become *de rigeur* in describing anything remotely out of the ordinary, and which most Americans pronounce 'arse-some'). The programmes were mildly informative to someone like me who remembers the decade well, but are so America-centric as to become very irritating after 10 minutes' or so of viewing. Even the fall of Communism was consigned to the last 10 minutes of one episode, seemingly having occurred as a result of the broadcasting of 'Dallas' in Romania and David Hasselhoff giving a concert atop the Berlin Wall.

Close Combat

This one is just an excuse to mimic violent computer games. A square-jawed, rough-hewn 'expert' in military combat techniques shows us how to take out a member of the Taliban, or storm a terrorist den, or neutralise anybody else you happen to have taken a dislike to.

Air Crash Investigation

Whenever this pops up on screen I can't take my eyes off it – I'm fascinated, like a rabbit before a stoat. Obviously, this is because I do such a lot of air travel myself. Each programme follows, in highly dramatic fashion (frequent repetition of frightening incidents, scary crescendos of discordant music) the progress of a flight that went wrong. Then the experts do their stuff, and conclude that it was either a) pilot error, b) terrorism, or c) a technical fault such as the tail of the plane falling off. It's compellingly melodramatic, although I can't say it's made me any more nervous of flying on commercial aircraft. I've always been perfectly fatalistic about this, I guess relying on those statistics that are regularly trotted out about air travel being much safer than driving your car, drinking beer, going to the toilet in the dark, etc...

****

I've been surfing the channels for about 45 minutes now, have really been served up some dire stuff, but it's still raining outside… night is closing in on Port of Spain… think I'll head back to Encore Westerns to see if Death Valley Days has finished…

Yes, it has! The first of two episodes of 'Wanted Dead or Alive' has just started. Here's Steve McQueen/Josh Randall riding across the prairie, he's taking into town some outlaw or other he's captured along the way. He's so cool and laconic I can almost feel relaxation oozing out of the television screen. I think he's feeling sympathetic towards his prisoner, maybe he thinks he didn't commit the crime for which he's going to be tried, and probably hanged. He knows that, somewhere along the way, the prisoner will try to make a getaway. He'll have to stop him, but somehow he's going to have to resolve all the moral, emotional and practical issues that are swirling around, by the end of the half-hour episode. Maybe they'll be resolved happily, maybe not. My guess is that the prisoner will get killed in his escape attempt – falling off a cliff, or something like that – and then right at the end, someone will gallop along from the town to announce they've found out he was not guilty, after all, and died in vain.

'He's the guy on his horse, the guy alone. He has his own code of ethics, his own rules of living.'

Before I started watching this series, I never really understood why Steve McQueen was known as 'king of cool'. In fact, being cool is the essential quality in all the heroes of the best of these series – Josh Randall, Cheyenne Bodie (Clint Walker) and Matt Dillon (James Arness) all have coolness in spades, even in the most desperate situations. This is perhaps the key fascination in watching them, along with the taut, no-nonsense pace of the scripts and screenplay. They really are admirable personalities, whose faultlessness contrasts so sharply with the human, often excusable, weaknesses in their adversaries on which the denouement of each episode depends. They dispense justice ruthlessly but even-handedly, fully subject to emotional conflict but always bound by the harsh rules of the world in which they live: Matt Dillon's words as he stalks through a windswept Boot Hill as a preface to each episode of 'Gunsmoke' is a perfect summary of the moral dilemma they constantly face:

'How many times I'd rather have argued than gone for guns…arguing doesn't fill any graves…when they draw their guns somebody's got to be around –on the law side.'

Anyway, to be more prosaic, I never tire of watching episodes of these series – even if, after a couple of months of tuning in to 'Encore Westerns', the same ones start to come round again. I've even fallen in love with one of the flawed heroines – a hunted woman protected by Cheyenne Bodie, who at the end of the episode in question (which I've now seen at least twice) shoots dead the evil husband who is stalking her, and is willing to face the consequences – a perfect example of 1950s feminism, Western style!

Kulture Shock - Part Two-and-a-half: The Liquidator

'Pawn Stars' may be lowbrow, but it's quite compelling viewing for someone like me who appreciates antiques....

I'm no longer in Sport-of-Pain, I'm in Kyiv, which is very different but in some ways for me very much the same… it's Sunday afternoon and I'm pretty bored… I've got the TV on again, it's a choice between 'Animal Planet', 'Discovery Channel', or the absolute dirge of 'Euronews' which 'aims to cover World News from a pan-European perspective', and makes one realise why the European Union is so, so dull. Anyway, I've settled on 'Discovery Channel' for the time being.

I'm watching a programme called 'The Liquidator'. It's a sort of downmarket 'Pawn Stars', if that's possible; a loudmouth, Jack-the-Lad American (Canadian?) who drives around buying and selling stuff. He is brash, altogether crass, always swearing a lot - 'beeped' out of course to respect the delicate sensitivities of the viewer, but when he gets excited the 'beeps' are interspersed so frequently between the non-swear-words that it's hard to know what he is actually talking about. His deeply unpleasant persona is pretty obviously one that the programme producers have primed because they think it's somehow going to appeal to viewers, and to some viewers, perhaps, somehow it does. But for me it is so irritating that after about 10 minutes I switch back to 'Animal Planet' which is all about vets: vets in Alaska, vets in Colorado, vets in just about every remote American state you can bring to mind.

I think I only kept watching 'The Liquidator' as long as I

did because, a few days ago, I watched part of a different episode – and could hardly believe what I was seeing, I was so shocked.

Not because of the 'beep' quotient, but the content of the episode. Being broadcast just six weeks before a US Presidential election at which the orange-dyed-haired, bullying, virulently racist Donald Trump is the Republican candidate, left me deeply troubled. A Donald Trump, let us recall, who wants to deport millions of Mexican immigrants, and who has declared his intent to ban all Muslims from entering the US of A. altogether, because he doesn't trust them not to suicide bomb Manhattan.

Permit me to describe the episode in question.

Mr. Liquidator has just bought himself a motorcycle and sidecar. He has paid a lot of money for it because he believes it to be German World War II vintage and therefore highly collectable. But he is not sure about it, so he calls in an expert he knows to check over its authenticity.

The expert gives him a nasty shock. It isn't authentic at all, it seems, but is a more recent Chinese-made copy. Mr. Liquidator is totally miffed, a sentiment I can identify with myself, having over the years bought more than one item of antique furniture which has turned out to be – well, fake, to put it bluntly.

'Whaddaya mean, (beeping) phoney?' Screams Mr. Liquidator. *'I mean, I paid **five thousand (beeping) dollars for this!** How'm I gonna make a (beeping) profit on it? I'm gonna (beep) that mother(beeper) that (beeping) sold it me!*

I'm gonna (beep) his ass! Whadda (beeping) (beeper)!'

After a while he calms down a little and tries to think of rational ways he can mitigate his loss rather than beeping someone about it. Maybe something can be done... the motorcycle needs some restoration, so he calls in a mechanic to have a look at it.

The mechanic is called Ali. He is very suave. He declares that in his opinion the motorcycle is genuine after all, and he can fix it up beautifully and make Mr. Liquidator a handsome profit.

'Oh yes,' he smiles, *'I can restore this. It can restore it beautiful! Mr. Liquidator, you be so happy when I done the job you be beaming from ear to ear – like this!'*

And Ali grins across the breadth of his swarthy, bearded, decidedly un-American-looking face...

But, the days pass by. The deadline by which Ali the olive-skinned is supposed to have delivered the restored motorcycle has passed. Cut to Mr. Liquidator in his office, calling Ali on his mobile phone. At this stage he is still relatively calm.

'Hi, Ali, this is Mr. Liquidator here. About the motorbike you're fixing for me. I need to know where you are with the repairs to that bike. Please get back to me and let me know what's going on. Bye.'

But there is no response, not to texts, not to emails, not to further calls.

'Hello again, Ali, Mr. Liquidator here. I <u>need to know</u> where you're at with the bike. I need the bike back immediately. So get back to me right away, OK? This is costing me money, man, so I want it back <u>right now.</u> Bye.'

But – still no reply.

'Ali, I need my (beeping) bike! What the (beep) are you (beeping) doing, man? If you don't (beeping) get back to me right away I'm gonna (beep) and (beeping) (beep) in your (beeping) (beeper). Bye.'

Nothing, nothing… so in the end Mr. Liquidator calls in the services of a repo man and they go round together to Ali's address (why Mr. L didn't think of doing this before is a mystery maybe only known to the programme's producers: maybe in the interests of dramatic effect?).

The rest is soon told. Initially, no response from Ali to the repeated shoutings and bangings on his front door, all recorded in wobbly-dramatic style by a cameraman following Mr. L and the repo man around his home. When Ali does respond he is initially aggressive, but then simply gives up and invites Mr. L. to repossess his merchandise – which he immediately does while uttering yet another chaplet of beeped-out expletives. End-of-story: American justice has prevailed, in this case against the dodgily-foreign if not actually Iranian perpetrator of a terrible crime against capitalism…

****

What is my problem with this? Well… imagine you are watching this broadcast in Toolallahoosa, Tennessee.

Imagine that you are a Donald Trump supporter – as I guess most inhabitants of Toolallahoosa, Tennessee actually are. Some of Donald's pithiest declarations concerning foreigners might come to mind…

"There were people cheering… where they have large Arab populations. They were cheering as the World Trade Center came down."

"I think, Islam hates us."

"We're going to knock the (beep) out of ISIS."

"The other thing with terrorists is you have to take out their families."

So, what are you going to be thinking? Maybe something like: *'…that Ali we've just seen – he ain't no true American, noooo way, he's a (beepin') A-Rab, man! He's only here 'cos those pinko spineless Democrats have set him loose in our great country. And look what he's doin', man! Him 'n' his kind's like rabid dogs, they need shootin' down, man, ain't no way we should be toleratin' (beeping) A-Rabs like him to be here among us…'*

I speculate, of course – but this is why I was shocked. Is 'Discovery Channel' somehow linked up to the Donald Trump presidential campaign? As propaganda for the Piggy-Faced One, it could hardly have broadcast anything more in-line with his thinking, or more in more timely fashion to support his appalling pre-election rhetoric.

Taking the wind out of my own sails, a little more online research told me that 'The Liquidator' is indeed Canadian not American: Jack-the-Lad hails from Vancouver. The programme was broadcast on an American TV channel, though… so for my money it just adds another nasty, xenophobic little element to what must surely be the nastiest, xenophobiciest US presidential election campaign ever.

Kulture Shock - Part Two-and-three-quarters: Intolerance and Absurdity

Tolerance/intolerance has been something of a theme in these musings. I've declared on several occasions that I'm becoming more tolerant, and less obsessive, as I get older. However, I must admit that this isn't always the case. Especially concerning things I regard as immoral, or absurd – like 'The Liquidator' – or like…

…some time ago, I think when I was staying at our UK home, a leaflet popped through the letterbox. It was from an insurance company (NPI), and it declared boldly on the front:

'An estimated 40% of people qualify for an increased retirement income due to poor health and lifestyle'.

It went on to give examples of this happy 40 percent: take Margaret (65): *'Margaret is overweight and a smoker, and takes medication for both high blood pressure and cholesterol daily… Margaret received enhanced annuity quotes offering on average 35% more annuity income.'*

Now, this strikes me as both immoral and absurd. Of course, I understand the principle: actuarily speaking, someone who is unhealthy has a reduced life expectancy, therefore the calculation is that more money can be paid out to that person as pension, because it will most likely be for a shorter period of time. But in an age when a healthy lifestyle is universally promoted and encouraged, how can it be that someone who persists with an <u>unhealthy</u> lifestyle is rewarded in comparison with someone who tries to be healthy (like me) in order to reduce the risk of dying early?

I don't know the answer to this conundrum. One reason we are urged to stay healthy is to limit the costs and pressure on national healthcare systems. Could it be possible to make some kind of counterbalance, in which healthy retired people perhaps receive a form of payback in relation to retired people who persist in smoking, drinking too much, sedentary behaviour, or whatever? Very complicated to administer, I suppose, but maybe not impossible, and surely more in line with modern-day thinking about lifestyle, healthcare costs, ageing populations, etc.

The alternative for me, I suppose, would be to stop my running and other forms of physical exercise, take up smoking, put on as much weight as possible, have a heart attack, then contact NPI (as it happens, part of my personal pension fund is managed by them) and follow the steps advocated in the brochure:

Step 1: *call 0845 301 0160*

Step 2: *'After an initial discussion Phoenix Customer Care can introduce you to an enhanced annuity provider....'*

Step 3: *'If you qualify... they will help you through the application process'.*

How perfectly simple! Since I suppose it would be in their interests to sign me up, would they have a scheme to keep me up to the mark in my unhealthy habits, thus inducing a second, ideally fatal heart attack that would put an end to my enhanced annuity and add to their enhanced profits?

Rip Solar – Interplanetary Agent

This is a little story submitted early in 2023 to a literary magazine which was publishing an edition with the theme 'solar'. It didn't get accepted.

When I was a boy in the 1960s, I subscribed to an illustrated comic called 'Ranger'. One of the comic-strip heroes who appeared in its pages was 'Rip Solar – Interplanetary Agent'.

Whatever induced Mr and Mrs Solar to call their little boy 'Rip'? Anyhow, young Rip grew up to be a typically British, square-jawed action hero, living in a futuristic world threatened successively by various malevolent extra-terrestrial civilisations, all of whose evil designs he managed to thwart with the help of his trusty sidekick, Burke. If I remember correctly, the strip didn't last very long. It wasn't particularly well-drawn, and conflicted with Ranger's other, much better presented and compelling sci-fi series, 'The Rise and Fall of the Trigan Empire'. When Ranger was taken over by the much less action-packed weekly 'Look and Learn' in 1967, it was dropped.

******

'Ranger', 'Lion', and 'Hotspur' - all the comics available to me in the early-to-mid 1960s had stirring-sounding names but Ranger was more erudite, including printed articles rather than just comic strips, and less-focused on the mythology of the Second World War, from a British perspective. I devoured these war stories as greedily as any of my little friends; of course, in the 1960s the Second

World War was quite a recent memory to our parents, many of whom had actively participated. Prior to 'Ranger', my favourite comic strip, in the 'Lion', I think, was entitled 'Captain Hurricane'. The captain in question was a huge, muscle-bound British Tommy who, during most of each week's offering, allowed himself to be pushed around sorely by the Germans, the 'Japs', or even the Italians (who, as all of us schoolboys knew, had the reputation of being cowards and not real fighters). Then, towards the end of the strip, something treacherous someone did to him would push him over the edge and he would go into what was always proclaimed by the story writer, in bold capitals, to be a 'RAGING FURY!!!'. At this point, seizing his Tommy Gun, a handful of grenades or whatever other weapons were to hand, Captain Hurricane would storm the enemy lines, machine-gunning and otherwise annihilating all enemy troops unfortunate enough to be in his way. Each episode ended in more or less the same manner.

The villainous enemies in this and other similar cartoon strips were a pretty inarticulate lot. The Germans' vocabulary was invariably limited to a few phrases: 'Donner und Blitzen', 'Gott in Himmel' and 'Britisher Pigdog' being the most common. The Japs were even more guttural, with 'Banzai!' and 'Aieee...'' (the latter being uttered while being blown to bits by a shell or grenade) being the only things they were generally capable of.

******

Sorry about all that – I wanted to get it off my chest. What, you readers must be asking yourselves, apart from the name of our eponymous hero (are heroes the only beings regularly described as 'eponymous'?) does this have to do with the theme 'solar'? Well, not very much. But to get back on track, permit me to describe my favourite episode of 'Rip Solar – Interplanetary Agent', entitled 'The Shining Planet'.

Even here, I suppose, my connection to the theme is rather thin. As everyone knows, the Sun is not a planet, but it does shine (sometimes) so perhaps I may be forgiven this little inconsistency. Anyway, this story concerns a race of super-beings who dwell on the (eponymous?) Shining Planet. For reasons that are never fully explained in the comic strip (which unfolds over several weekly issues) the Shining Planet approaches Planet Earth and completely destroys everything in an apocalyptic tsunami, only Solar and Blake being left alive. The Super-Beings, who are tall, identical, egg-shaped-headed creatures with benign expressions, are *incredibly* intelligent and travel around on small hover-discs that are propelled purely by the force of their minds. Solar and Blake vainly attempt to evade them.

"The two space-beings must be here somewhere, but their intelligence level is so feeble it is hard to detect unless we think-listen quietly..."

Eventually they are captured: 'The vast mental power suddenly unleashed on Solar and Blake was of such smashing violence that they were both knocked unconscious. And when they recovered...'

"Welcome to Ultima, the planet built by the energy of thought. You see around you the result of a million years of increasing mind power."

Solar angrily berates the Super-Beings for having so wantonly destroyed Planet Earth. But the Chief Super-Being tells him all is not lost, they will undo the damage they have done...

Solar: "It is too late. Millions have died. Worlds have been wrecked."

Chief S-B: "We shall turn back time. The total mind strength of my race will be applied to the task..."

'In the next instant, the strange beings begin to fade away...'

'Time ran backwards like a film in reverse, and the destroyed world began to reassemble itself...'

And Solar and Blake find themselves back on Earth at the moment the cataclysm occurred, with no recollection of anything that has happened since. Solar is sitting at a dressing table combing his hair, in preparation for a ceremony in a vast, modernistic edifice in a London of the future...

******

I'd like to think there is some resonance in Rip Solar, Interplanetary Agent, in the world of today. I don't mean to say I think the Sun could somehow approach the Earth, or more plausibly that the Earth could approach the Sun, causing our planet to explode like a hot chestnut amongst the embers. Nor that the Sun is inhabited by a super-race that, like the inhabitants of the Shining Planet, could deliberately bring about our destruction for reasons unknown.

But, could *global warming* create something as cataclysmic as complete planetary destruction? This *is* more plausible, perhaps… in which case the super-intelligent Super-Beings confronted by Rip Solar could be seen as a proxy for *human beings*, becoming so technologically advanced as to bring mankind to an end, in spite of itself.

As for Rip, who could he be? Greta Thunberg?

Please Have My Room, Mr President

George W. Bush – remember him? He was the absolute paragon of joke American Presidents, until someone else came along...

The Holiday Inn in Dar-es-Salaam, Tanzania, is a very attractive, comfortable hotel. It stands not far from the centre of town, in the pleasant district of tree-lined boulevards and elegant public buildings between the sea front and the commercial district. It was only built within the last few years; it definitely wasn't there when I was working in Dar-es-Salaam 10 years ago, at the end of the 1990s. The interior is tasteful and original, featuring a Zanzibari theme with latticework, marble fountains, rich brocade upholstery and deeply carved, iron-bound chests and other furniture in the lobby and corridors. The staff, in their stylish East African style uniforms, are friendly and helpful. Behind the hotel there is access to the National Botanical Gardens, a little run-down but still a relaxing place to go for a stroll on a Sunday afternoon.

I was looking forward to staying there earlier this year, when I travelled out to Dar to conduct a short organisational review project for the Tanzania Ministry of Local Self-Government. I duly arrived and checked in at reception – a booking had been made for me by my client, the Local Government Reform Unit. The reservation was only for the first three days of my scheduled stay of two weeks – however, I wasn't too surprised about this, as I knew that at some time during the stay I would have to travel up-country to Dodoma for a couple of days, Dodoma being the location of Tanzania's Parliament and the headquarters of the

Ministry of Local Self-Government.

It was only the next day, when I was told that the Dodoma trip was not scheduled until my second week, that I realised the true reason for my abridged booking. A US Presidential Delegation, George W. Bush and all, was coming to Tanzania at the weekend for the first stage of an East-to-West across-Africa tour. The Holiday Inn had been block-booked, from two days prior to George W.'s arrival until the day of departure, by the United States Embassy to accommodate *just part* of the huge entourage accompanying the great man himself.

"I'm sorry, we really can't help you," said the apologetic receptionist when I pleadingly tried to extend my booking, *"and all the other places where we usually redirect people to in such circumstances have been booked up as well. If I were you, I'd try and make some arrangements as quickly as you can to find somewhere else to stay."*

****

My client counterpart in the Reform Unit (not an American) was pretty pissed off when I told her this news. She started phoning round immediately, but the receptionist's warning proved correct – finding *anywhere* available in Dar at this time was a real problem. Even the beach hotels out of town had little or no availability. Eventually, however, my counterpart discovered that some accommodation was available at a small place not too far from the Unit's offices, at that intriguingly named Tanzanian institution, the *Q-Bar.*

****

The Q-Bar... the name brought back some vivid memories of my earlier time in Dar. The Q-Bar... I remembered it actually opening for business sometime during my previous visit, soon becoming a popular haunt of locals and expatriates alike on Friday and Saturday nights. It was, effectively, a sports bar, run by a Scandinavian couple, I think, situated on the Msasani Peninsula, the upmarket end of Dar across the Solander Bridge and away from the bustling centre of town. Now it was apparently a guest house as well, with the guest rooms on the upper levels of the building in which the bar was located. I well recalled myself having had some jolly times there with other expatriates of my acquaintance, drinking beer, playing games of pool and watching football matches on the wide-screen TVs. I particularly recalled having watched the 1998 World Cup Final there (France three, Brazil nil) when in the midst of the party atmosphere a large, half-drunk Brazilian wearing a 'Ronaldo' jersey became aggressive and had to be ejected into the street.

Not having much, as if by any other choice, I asked my counterpart to go ahead with the booking, and looked forward to installing myself in my new accommodation with much interest, but some trepidation. The Q-Bar was considerably cheaper than the Holiday Inn, only about 30 US dollars per night, I think. Obviously, this meant that the rooms would probably be rather basic. I expected that there would surely be rather a lot of noise, especially at weekends. I also remembered that the Q-Bar had previously been and probably still was the hang-out of flocks of hopeful young Tanzanian gals, on the lookout for gullible, drunk or desperate expats with whom to establish harmonious relationships. These interesting young ladies, I suspected, might provide me with certain challenges in making passage from the front porch of the bar to the stairs at the back, or even the front door of my hotel room. However...

Disappointment and dismay are related to expectation, I suppose, and in this case most of my misgivings proved (relatively) unfounded. My room at the Q-Bar was very spacious, if not rather sparse, and on an upper level so that the decibel quotient was not particularly intrusive except on the Friday night when a live band was playing in the bar. The young ladies were friendly but not persistent: a smile, a wave and a scurrying retreat proved sufficient to see them off. There *were* some unexpected inconveniences: for example, the supply of water to the shower (an essential creature comfort in dusty, humid Dar) was very erratic, usually being little more than a trickle at the beginning which gurgled away to a few tepid drops after just a minute or two of showering. The Q-Bar had its own generator to cut in during the frequent power cuts, but this only had enough juice to supply electricity to the bar itself, with its large multiple TV screens, if the grid went down after nightfall. There was nothing to be done but go and drink in the bar, or sit (or literally sweat!) it out until normal service was resumed by TANELEC.

****

But what of the Presidential Delegation?

I saw nothing of it, myself. I went to Dodoma, and came back, and didn't go anywhere near the centre of town when the great event actually took place. I was given plenty of feedback from others, however. The local newspapers had been excitedly full of the three, or four, day visit just before it occurred and at its beginning, particularly as Mr President announced a half-million-dollar grant to the nation to help with some public health issues and uttered a few well-choreographed words of greeting in Kiswahili. But the mood rapidly turned sour. There seemed to be some uncertainty, after all, concerning whether the grant really was a grant, or whether there were certain strings attached. Despite George W.'s formal attempts to 'break the ice' with his hosts, the general deportment of his entourage was insular, arrogant and bullying. The Holiday Inn and whatever other accommodation that had been booked proved insufficient, I understood that a number of other hotels were commandeered at the last minute, with the rightful residents simply being turned out of their rooms for the Americans with little to no warning.

George W. Bush! Don't we all *love* him! So genial, such a lovable fool – did he ever get *anything* right, while his NeoCon friends were busy winning the war in Iraq, and feathering their own nests? Thousands of deaths, one failed war and one failed global economy later...

****

The Q-Bar was really more a hostel than a hotel. I only had a couple of days left in Tanzania when I returned from Dodoma, and I couldn't face going back to my power cuts and dribbling apology of a shower, so I tried another place instead. This too proved to be rather quirky. It was a spanking-brand-new edifice with a huge sports centre attached, also in Msasani, and with a sort of Las Vegas-cum-

Ancient-Roman theme: all marble, statuary and gold-plated fittings (it was called 'The Coliseum'). I spent a comfortable enough night there, and enjoyed a vigorous workout on the treadmills and weights machines in the fitness centre.

Come to think of it, Dar-es-Salaam overall is a rather quirky place: full of contrasts, scruffy, friendly and easy-going in the sunshine. It also *does* seem to have more than its fair share of odd hotels! The oddest of all, which may or may not still exist (I stayed in it over 10 years ago, when I first arrived in Dar in the 1990s) was the Oyster Bay Hotel. Owned, I was told, by an idiosyncratic Welshman, it was a rambling, half-constructed edifice in a prime, ocean-view location on Msasani. The grounds – half landscaped, half derelict – were the home of a diverse menagerie of animals and birds. The restaurant was closed. The rooms, full of ornate antique Zanzibari furniture and assorted vermin, were cold and unhygienic. One could relax in the dirty yellow water of the elaborate tropical swimming pool, with its ferns, rocks and waterfalls, which was next to that part of the complex which was still, quite literally, a building site. Whether or not the building works were ever completed, a large part of the structure mysteriously burned down some years later, although at that time the business somehow still kept going.

Hmm… nostalgic about all this I may be, but if I ever go back again to Dar I'll definitely head for the Holiday Inn!

What I Don't Talk About When Not Talking About Running with the Kenyans

Another interesting title, no? This little memoir is about my own personal running experiences but was generated by my reading of three books: all of them about running. *My* title is an amalgam of their titles, as below. All of these books were read with interest since I am myself a runner. All are very different, but all provide sufficient food for the thought, that I'll attempt gracefully to regurgitate in these musings.

The first book: '*What I talk about when I talk about running*'. A fairly short (180 pages) memoir by the celebrated Japanese writer, Haruki Murakami. According to my daughter - who gave me the book - he's the most popular writer of fiction in Japan, and certainly his stylish, well-balanced prose, and his clarity of thought shine brightly throughout. I enjoyed reading it at the beginning, but eventually became a bit bored: after all, there's only so much one can say about one's thoughts when engaged on a long-distance run. It all became a bit navel-contemplative in the end, to the extent that getting through the last few chapters of the book for me was quite gruelling: like the latter stages of running a half-marathon, in fact.

Second book: '*Running with the Kenyans*'. A (self-confessed) moderately talented Brit runner decamps with his family to Iten, the mountainous region of Kenya that produces so many of the world's top distance runners - to try and find out what makes them so. '*What can be their secret?*' the author, Adharanand Finn, asks. '*Discover the secrets of the fastest people on Earth*' the book frontispiece proclaims, in response. In fact, Finn of the Unpronounceable

First Name eventually concludes that there isn't actually a secret, more a combination of specific factors: running barefoot, altitude, starting at an early age (running to school each day to avoid getting a licking for being late), a balanced diet, and above all, the dedication to become a successful international runner (this being the gateway to comparative riches). The one thing Adhar...thingummy studiously doesn't mention throughout is the 'D' word: '*Doping is commonplace in Kenyan athletics*' according to a recent report launched following the World Anti-doping Agency's (WADA) threat to ban Kenya from the Olympics due to the high incidence of its athletes failing drugs tests. Hmm... several of these athletes are ones mentioned in the book, if not actual running companions of Adhar...whatshisname. Was he perhaps a little naïve during his six months in the Kenya Rift Valley? Anyway, I found the book pretty entertaining in part, just because it was so charmingly naïve concerning the East African lifestyle, and mentality, in contrast to that of a Brit. I encountered the same cultural shock in the past, while working on projects in Tanzania, Rwanda, and elsewhere in the region.

Third book: '*The Runner's Handbook*'. A lengthy and exhaustive manual produced by a leading US running coach (Bob Glover), aimed mostly at the beginner to running and jam-packed with valuable information and advice. It's actually very useful, it really does tell you everything you need to know and sets out a clear step-by-step approach for anyone wanting to take up running: how to build up your fitness from scratch, how to derive maximum pleasure from physical activity, how to progress systematically from 'beginner' to 'intermediate' to 'master runner' (Glover's own definitions). There are lots of useful facts about aerobic fitness, safety measures, staying motivated and so forth. To a non-US reader, what rather grates, however, is the chummy, false-bonhomie style of writing so typical of American authors: *'It's just great to keep your fellow-runners motivated. Whenever I pass an older guy running up a hill, I always give him a lift: 'hey, old timer! You're looking great! You're in great shape!'* Huh! I guess I'm an 'old timer' now! If anyone said that to me, I'd be tempted to sock him in the mouth.

****

Same subject matter, all very different. One trend in all three that stands out is – obsessiveness. All the authors claim - each in their own way - not to take things too seriously; to ensure that running is no more than a part (albeit an important one) of an overall balanced lifestyle. They are not very convincing in this, however, the veil is very thin, and sometimes wafts away altogether. For example: Murakami's self-proclaimed uncompetitive approach occasionally morphs into jubilation over how he has passed someone, or beaten another runner in a race. Monsieur Adharanand's Mission in Africa is obsessive in itself, and although he does genuinely seem to take account of the culture shock he inflicted on his family, he too sometimes lapses into glory mode: how he, such a modestly talented individual after all, has run faster than someone else. As for Bob Glover, he declares at the outset that any runner should aim to get out at least five times a week, and ideally six times a week, if he's at all serious about it. Haruki Murakami royally exceeds this target: he claims to run every day for at least an hour per day. But for how many more modestly intentioned - would-be - runners is this target attainable? Glover elaborately explains how, by managing one's work and home life schedules, six-day-per-week running should not be a problem for anyone. I'm not convinced, however!

All the same, I think that obsessiveness and competitiveness is an inherent part of running, however good or bad at it one might be. Take me for example: I don't subscribe to the five or six days per week ideology, but I do aim to run at least three times a week, and get quite twitchy if I don't meet my target. And although my competitive running has been confined to a few local half-marathons and road races, and although I've never aspired to finish higher than half-way up a field, just like Finn and Murakami, I've always taken a certain secret pleasure in overtaking someone else who's scrambling along at a slower pace than me.** Maybe it's just the adrenalin rush? I don't think I'm an inherently aggressive person, but I have sometimes become seriously aggressive when bothered by something during a run: excitable dogs, or inconsiderate motorists; see below for these and other examples).

****

I've been running regularly now for over 20 years, and my approach to it has changed periodically over this timescale.

**The opposite sentiment, of course, when I'm overtaken by someone else. I once got passed in a race by a man who was running with a dog on a leash. I passed them back later when the dog stopped for a pee, but within a few hundred metres they were off and striding away from me again. And then there was the time, more recently, when running around the Savannah in Port of Spain, Trinidad, I was overtaken by a woman running along while pushing a baby in a pushchair...

I started in late 1997, shortly after leaving the Czech Republic where we'd lived the past three-and-a-half years. I can't really remember why I got started; I Just wanted to keep fit, I suppose. I remember doing shortish runs in exotic places where I was subsequently working, for instance in Grenada, and Dar-es-Salaam: (where initially, being unsure about the security of running around the dusty roads of the Msasani Peninsula, I confined myself to the grounds of the hotel where I was staying - much to the amusement of other guests).

Later I went through a phase where I did quite a lot of road races, and, as above, a couple of half-marathons. I always did try to finish as high up the field as possible, but never did anything spectacular in this respect. I was very satisfied with my fastest half-marathon time, however (one hour 45 mins. exactly), and I suppose overall I would categorise myself as slightly above average - more than a jogger, but not capable of bringing down my time much below five minutes per kilometre - and therefore way, way short of being categorised as an elite runner. I've never been tempted to try and run a marathon, to my mind that really does require too much commitment. But at my peak (in terms of enthusiasm, at least) I did start to think about ways of improving my running through eating more appropriately, joining an athletics club, or whatever. But eventually, I got fed up with road racing. I was never really taken by in the exhilaration (competitiveness?) of it, so extolled by Bob Glover and others. Besides which, participating in organised races in France requires the ridiculous process of obtaining a medical certificate each year, which has to be submitted beforehand in order to participate. A stupid formality requiring usually no more than doing a few knee bends in front of a doctor, and the taking of one's pulse before and after, but sufficient of a bore to dampen the enthusiasm of someone already as half-hearted about it as me.

Despite this, more recently I did go through a phase of trying to improve my running speeds. It went like this: on some of my more regular running routes: (almost all of which involve a circuit from home, around the nearby lanes and tracks, of varying distance from 5-12 km) I got into the habit of doing periodic little sprints (I don't suppose Mo Farah would call them that!), then taking my time at the end of the run to see if I could improve. A kind of self-competitiveness: could I reduce my route - Masigné / Coutanciere / Le Saz / Le Parrelais circuit to under 30 minutes? Or Pont du Forge / Verriere / Le Panettiere / Gergaudiere to less than 50? Some of these routes involve quite serious climbs (Cote du Saz is particularly demanding) and I always had a strong sense of satisfaction whenever I beat my best time. 'Hills are your friend' someone once said to me, referring to how they can dramatically increase one's aerobic fitness; he was a cyclist not a runner, but the principle is the same!

But now, I've given up all attempts at speed running and have decided to just toddle round at a pace that suits me, like any old semi-fit jogger. Is it because I'm getting older? I don't think so, just finding it more enjoyable and relaxing. I think that, up to a point, I've finally got a bit bored with running, and have just decided to take it a bit easier. How to maintain my motivation? I've thought about taking a backpack, doing longer, slower runs, exploring new places.

Something between running and rambling; stopping whenever I feel like it to enjoy the scenery and take a little light refreshment before carrying on. I'll probably give it a try, if my old knees will stand it as I progress through my 60s.

****

So, why *do* I do it? Very often, I don't feel like it. The motivation is always lowest at the very beginning of a run; I always tell myself I'll feel OK once I get going, and this is almost always the case. Motivation... there's the fitness thing, and the desire I've always had to explore the countryside where I live. And the undoubted feeling of moral achievement as well as and physical wellness one feels on finishing a run... but really, I think it's actually just become a habit that I can't kick (hahaha). What do I think (not talk) about when I'm running? Nothing in particular; sometimes about going fishing, sometimes about what I'm going to have for my dinner. Sometimes I just cogitate away rhythmically at some pointless calculation: *'If a brick weighs a pound and half a brick, how much does a brick weigh?'*. Things like this can carry me through several kilometres. How long can I keep going? I don't know the answer to that either; I suspect that one day those previously mentioned dodgy knees will call time on things. But I hope not too soon as I'm sure I'd like to be still running into my 70s. Not just a question of personal pride, I suppose at the back of my mind I'm hoping I can somehow prolong my life by keeping as fit as possible. I know there are no guarantees about this, but I'll do whatever I can to increase the possibility of making it up to 100.

Now to describe some of my running problems:

Number one: dogs. I've never been bitten by a dog when out running, apart from the odd little nip from some crazy, undersized mutt, that I could have kicked into the ditch if I'd chosen to. Over-enthusiastic dogs have, however, sometimes been a problem. They want to run along with you; they frolic and bark and then inevitably get tangled up in your legs, and you fall over. Then they go, 'Woof! Woof! Woof!' and lick your face. It's important to take this in your stride (another non-intended joke), make sure doggie is reunited with its owner, and run on.

What's more of a problem are dogs that want to come along with you, and won't stop. Once, running along a minor road, a large but clearly juvenile doggie came lolloping out of a driveway, and started prancing around me, charging up the road, down the road, across the road, all over the road, in fact. He was totally happy and excited, just wouldn't go back home. This became a problem when the minor road joined a major road. Doggie didn't care about the traffic, he seemed to regard playing a game of romps with cars as just part of the fun of the thing. It was so dangerous, in the end I just had to turn round and escort doggie back home. Clearly it had happened before. The owner wearily hauled him off and locked him in the house until I'd put enough distance between me and him to continue safely.

Number two: insects. Especially in summer, I quite frequently have the horrible experience of aspirating a small flying insect into my windpipe. It really is awful! There I am, gasping and choking and trying to cough the nasty thing up. Usually I stop for a few minutes, until it's liquidised in my gullet and I'm feeling better, then I carry on. Once, recently, I aspirated two insects during the same run. The second time, I was looking so horrible and wheezy, a passing motorist stopped to check if I was OK!

Number three: falling over. This happens not **too** frequently, but quite regularly. Tree roots can be a problem when running along woodland tracks, but having had a few tumbles I'm quite careful of them now. Most of my falls simply occur due to dragging a foot a bit, or catching my toe on the ground, and over I go. More worrying, sometimes an ankle or a knee gives way – I don't really know why. My last little accident (about nine months ago) was really what convinced me to stop my 'sprinting'. I hurt my knee quite badly. I'm now much more careful than I was previously, especially when running downhill. I expect I'll be down in the dust again sometime soon, however, you can't be ultra-careful where you place your feet all of the time.

Number four: cars. I always run facing the traffic, which you're recommended to do. Most motorists are pretty careful and give you a wide berth, and sometimes they'll or slow down/stop altogether if there's another vehicle behind you, coming the other way. I'm generally scrupulously polite when motorists treat me with such consideration, but on the other hand, I get quite excited (adrenaline again?) when someone comes too close. Two incidents come to mind: once, when getting to a zebra crossing just before a roundabout, an approaching car slowed down just as I was about to cross. When I stepped out, the car just kept on going, the driver (a middle-aged woman) was slowing down for the roundabout, not for me. I banged angrily on the roof of the car as I jumped out of the way, but the driver didn't look very apologetic. I've had to learn the hard way that (unlike in the UK) French drivers don't necessarily give way to pedestrians at zebra crossings.

The other incident was more scary, probably the only time I've come perilously close to being seriously injured or killed when out running. I was proceeding along a straight but fairly narrow road (as usual against the traffic), when I heard a car approaching from behind; but wasn't worried as I knew it was on the other side of the road. What I didn't know was that said car was being overtaken by another car, just as the two of them came up to me. I felt a rush of air as the overtaking car flew past. If I'd stepped a little to my right at that moment (again I was running in France) I might very probably have been hit. I gave the driver an extravagant 'V' sign, but by that time he was way off and down the road. I don't suppose he would have cared very much anyway.

Number five: weather. Much less scary, this – generally I don't mind running in bad weather – rain, cold, fog, or whatever, although here again I've become a little more picky lately, than I used to be. One problem I have is, that wearing glasses, they tend to steam up quite a lot in certain climatic conditions, particularly the combination of cold and humidity. Rain by comparison is less of a problem. I'm quite used to running in the tropics, where the heat and humidity means it's only really feasible to run at dusk or (preferably, - if I can get out of bed at 5.30 a.m.) - at daybreak. Even at these times it's quite easy to become dehydrated after quite a short time. If King Kong came along at the end of one of my tropics runs, picked me up, and squeezed me like an orange, he wouldn't get much juice out of me!

****

Apart from these fairly regular problems, a few other odd incidents come to mind when I review my running career.

My highest ever race finish

Once, when working in Macedonia, I decided to enter a race. This was being organised by the local athletics association, and the event I was qualified for (the veterans' race) was only about 1500 metres along the banks of the River Vardar in Skopje. I'd have liked to participate in one of the longer races on the programme, but when I enquired, I was told no, I was only eligible for the specific race that met my categorisation.

So, I turned up on the wide, flat stretch of riverbank where the event was due to start. There didn't seem to be anyone else around. Eventually, another runner of about my age turned up. As he was Macedonian, communication with him was rather difficult, but I gathered he was a retired Macedonian Air Force Officer. After a while, we decided to set off in the direction down river where we supposed the finish line to be. The finish did, in fact, prove to be underneath one of the bridges spanning the river downstream. As we approached, my companion proposed 'sprint?', so we raced the last hundred yards or so. I was edged out on the line and so finished second (and last).

I was presented with a certificate for my performance. Proof indeed that I finished second, but not last. I still have it. I showed it to my work colleagues the next day, who were at first mightily impressed, but then laughed when I explained the circumstances. I remember also being asked at the finish by one of the race organisers, 'no drugs?'. Unfortunately, I forgot to do my blood doping beforehand, otherwise assuredly I'd have finished first.

Passing blood

Talking of blood, about 10 years ago I had a few instances of passing blood during, or just after a run. A couple of times in Macedonia, in fact, and a couple of other times as well. It hasn't happened again more recently, however.

Naturally I was rather worried and went to see a specialist about it when back home in France.

The specialist was a real enthusiast. He told me straight away he didn't think it was anything serious – probably just a rupture of a small blood vessel in my bladder – but he made me do a series of very curious tests, anyhow. The first of these involved me pissing into a special kind of toilet, that a sensor to detect the flow ('debit') of my urine, recording this on a graph. The specialist excitedly showed me that my 'debit' was not too good, possibly indicating prostate problems. So he booked me up for another, more elaborate test.

I should have known this was going to be something very extraordinary when, a couple of days before the test, I went to the pharmacy to collect the required equipment This was something in a long, thin box, the shape of a box for a neon tube….

When I turned up for the appointment, I was told to strip off down to my socks. The 'object' was removed from its box: it proved to be a long sort of syringe-thing. I was given a local anaesthetic, and the end of the syringe was inserted into my willy, and then a special fluid was injected into my bladder. It was explained to me that the fluid would show up on a special monitor, so they could work out what the problem was.

'Assurement, vous sentirez l'envie de pisser,' said the anesthetician, 'mais il ne faut pas! C'est une liquid speciale pour qu'on peut surveiller comment l'urine sort de votre vaissie…'

I was standing on a special platform in a darkened room, then instructed to relieve myself at the required moment once the piss-flow-monitoring-machine was turned on. Lots of excited whisperings from the specialist and his staff, as they observed me urinating. At the end, they explained to me that the problem was nothing to do with my prostate, but rather that the exit tube from my bladder was rather narrow. The things one can learn about one's anatomy!

I was prescribed some pills to sort out the problem in the short term, but the specialist strongly advised me to have a corrective operation to sort things out on a permanent basis. I didn't fancy this, and have never had the operation. Strangely, however, the problem I had beforehand of wanting to wee very frequently, has improved greatly. I was always convinced it was mainly something psychological, probably something to do with wetting my pants regularly when I was an infant, and not wanting to own up about it.

Hash Runs

After this rather elaborate story, something simpler. I've written before about Hash Runs – those supreme expressions of British expatriate culture - and how much I loathe all the silly fun and games that follow a run (described by me as 'sub-rugby club culture'). Adharanand Finn too describes participating in a Hash Run during his time in Kenya, and is also very contemptuous of them; albeit for different reasons: fat, unfit people, all very slow, stupid expatriates confusing the locals, not real running at all. Well, he has a point, although to my mind, anyone who takes up running – however fat or unfit they are, however often they do it, – deserves a little more respect. I've done a few Hash Runs in Tanzania and Bangladesh respectively, and if you can stand all the post-running frivolities they are, after all, quite fun, and a refreshing change once in a while from just pounding around on your own.

Getting pumped up

I've already given some examples of losing my rag when out running, the car incidents in particular. I really do think the adrenaline rush makes one more intolerant of people getting under one's feet, and susceptible to bursts of rage. Although I've become much more tolerant than I used to be. Once or twice in the past, I've nearly got into punch-ups with people I felt were getting in my way, in one way or another, and sometimes on reflection I've had to conclude that it was mostly me being intolerant, than them being inconsiderate that caused the flashpoint.

****

So there we are, my own little contribution to the mass of literature about running, of which the books I described at the beginning are, I have no doubt, but three of many examples. I only hope that my own reflections come across as rather different from the mainstream of writers on this subject! Nevertheless, I leave the last word to Bob Glover:

"Running... allows us to discover our bodies and ourselves. This has an immediate effect on our self-esteem. Establishing goals and then reaching them... results in feeling of control over one's life – an important sense in a society that too often feels like it is controlling us."

In Memory of Mr Harry Cotterill

To reach Bear Pond, it is necessary to take the steep road out of the Derwent Valley at Whatstandwell and climb steadily for several miles. The pond itself, though high up in the Derbyshire hills, is in a sheltered, peaceful spot; it is surrounded by a plantation of conifers which form a protective screen, and although the west wind is often to be heard on stormy days rushing through the treetops, it rarely more than ruffles the surface of the water. About two-and-a-half acres in area, the pond is in the shape of a long, widening sleeve with a grassy dam wall at the widest end, and shallows at the other. There is a tiny island in the middle where, each year, a few Canada geese come to make their nests.

The first time I visited the pond to fish, I met Mr Harry Cotterill. It was a warm, still day in late spring; the fluffy buds were out on the sallow bushes at the water's edge, bees hummed in the depths of the conifer plantation. A bulky, angular figure in tweedy clothing, he was leaning on a shooting-stick at the dam wall end looking out into the sunlight across the water, his fishing rod propped up idly against the branches of a willow bush nearby. He gave us a nod as we walked up to him.

"Morning. Beautiful day, isn't it? Wonderful to be out on such a morning."

He told us he lived in Belper, further down the valley, alone now since his wife had died.

"Never go fishing anywhere else, you know. Been coming

192

here ever since the club had it. It's marvellous."

He nodded his head again, thrusting his thick, bulbous nose into the breeze, narrowing his eyes and sniffing happily at the warm spring air.

"Yes… been coming here for 30-odd years now. My wife used to come with me before she passed on, you know. We'd come up here for the day and make a picnic of it! It's marvellous. I'm over 80 now, but I still come here as often as I can."

We, the younger men, smiled politely at him without really listening. All the time, our eyes were scanning the water. Was that the plop of a rising trout under the bushes in the far corner? Perhaps the best place to fish would be in the shallows at the top where the stream ran in? Already, we were pulling our fly lines through our fingers, screwing together sections of our rods, trying to think which pattern of fly would be likely to bring success. At the first opportunity we were off, striding purposefully along the bank to reach our preferred spot. Our fly rods swished to and fro through the air, our knees were wetted as we crouched down in the marsh grass, the better to approach our rising fish. If we looked up from the water at all, Mr Cotterill would still be there, in the same spot, perched on his shooting stick by the water's edge. He rarely seemed to be bothered to reach for his fishing rod. He seemed quite content just to sit there, snuffling in the air, looking out across the water.

We visited the pond several times over succeeding years, always in the spring or early summer. Usually, the fishing was good. The place came to have a certain magic that made itself present in the warmth of the sun permeating the soft, brown earth, the peaty smell of the marsh grass, the drone of bees. Often, we would meet Mr Cotterill, always sitting in the same place, always wearing the same tweedy clothes, always ready with a word or two in his broad Derbyshire accent. He never did care much about catching anything. He was merged into the place, a brown figure you expected to see there as much as you expected to see the sluice gates of the dam or the yellow, fluffy buds on the willow bushes in spring.

One winter, a fishing club circular contained the announcement that Mr Harold Cotterill of Belper, a member for 34 years, had died peacefully in his sleep. No more would he be seen at Bear Pond, but the club was proposing to erect there a bench inscribed to his memory, near the place where he always used to stand. And there it is, by the water's edge, a wooden bench, the sort that you see in parks and public gardens,   inscribed:

'In memory of Mr Harry Cotterill, 1898-1983, a member of the club since its founding in 1949'

***

How long does a wooden bench last? I went up to Bear Pond recently, in late autumn, with my wife and baby daughter: no-one else there, of course, at this time of year after the fishing season had closed. It was a grey, windy day, with big rain-filled clouds scudding across the sky above, but it still felt warm around the pond behind its protective screen of trees. The baby I was holding in my arms, wrapped up in her sleeping bag, turned her head sleepily round and gazed with big, limpid eyes at the trickle of water bubbling from the sluice gates into the stream below. The bench – it too seemed to be merged into the landscape, rather as Mr Cotterill himself had always seemed to be. How long would it last? Would it be preserved, perhaps for centuries, by the peaty soil on which it stood – rather like the bodies of primitive men found preserved after centuries in peat bogs?

Somehow, I doubted it. Probably, the ghost of Harry Cotterill would only be there as long as men came there to fish, to sit on his bench and eat their lunchtime sandwiches while watching the ripples spreading across the water of the pond. But is that not sufficient of a memorial for any man?

Books

What's the worst book you've ever read?

The worst book I've *never* read (because it was so bad, I simply couldn't get through more than about two paragraphs) was called *'Master of Middle Earth'*. It was a book my father acquired, presumably thinking it was a biography of JRR Tolkien. It had a nice photograph of him on the cover - sitting in a Lord-of-the-Rings-like woodland dell - looking antediluvian and benign, but yet somehow supremely omnipotent: a bit like Gandalf, in fact.

When I dipped into it, I soon discovered that it wasn't a biography at all, but an elaborate exercise in sophistry. Written by some American crank called Paul H Kocher, it painstakingly revealed all the hidden complexities and significances that its author saw buried away in *'The Lord of the Rings'*. All of which he considered to have enormous consequences for the future of the planet, and of mankind. He used the word 'cosmic' a lot. The book was actually unreadable; complete gobbledygook! The crank's literary style being to throw as many long words into as many long sentences as possible, without actually saying anything coherent at all. Without wishing to blow my own trumpet too much, I think I can say that I have enough brains to understand quite complex arguments, if I put my mind to it. But in the case of this book, although I tried quite hard, I could almost feel my brains bubbling away like scrambled egg inside my head with all the fruitless mental effort:

'Tolkien is here facing a joint literary-philosophical imperative... if the guiding hand is really to guide effectively, it must have power to control events, yet not so much as to take away from the people acting them out the capacity for

196

moral choice... so Tolkien cannot allow his cosmic order to be
a fixed, mechanistic, unchangeable chain of causes and
effects. The order must be built flexibly around creaturely free
will and possible personal providential interventions from on
high.'

You see? I don't actually possess my father's copy anymore. It
must have been disposed of after he died when I was clearing
the house of all his and my mother's personal effects. Along
with several hundredweight worth of other books, (for my
father believed almost anything in print was of venerated
status, and he had a magpie-like instinct to accumulate reading
material that was hugely obscure, and of absolutely no
commercial value) it was wheeled away from the house in a
barrow, by a man who owned a junk shop somewhere on the
outskirts of Sheffield. He seemed pleased, at least I guess he
was going to have fun sorting through the enormous load of
books about art, books about architecture, books about
literature, books about just about anything and everything as
long as obscure. Since he got them for nothing, I suppose he
could also hope to make a little money out the (probably) tiny
percentage of them he managed to sell on to some other
aficionado (with a magpie-like mind, and a few spaces left on
his or her bookshelf).

****

I'm being curmudgeonly, as usual. These books (possibly
including *'Master of Middle Earth'*) must have brought my
father a good deal of pleasure over the years: pleasure in
reading them, criticising them, even just contemplating them –
and when I think about it, I, myself have an albeit smaller but
very eclectic collection of well-loved volumes that I frequently
dip into for amusement and mental solace: my R. S. Surtees

collection; my now backless copy of *'Fishing with Mr Crabtree in all Waters'*; *'Peakland'*, a quaintly-1950s Derbyshire guide by the curiously-named writer, Crichton Porteous. When at home I habitually turn to one of these - among others - to settle down for a happy half-hour or so; to chuckle over the harum-scarum escapades of Jorrocks, or Mr Sponge; or relive fond memories of days out fishing or hiking in the Peak District, or whatever.

And yet - without being iconoclastic, one could certainly say that there are far, far too many books in the world. So many of them are outdated, or irrelevant; or just simply rubbish, yet they all physically exist in sum total: a crushing weight of cardboard, ink and paper weighing down enormously on planet Earth. Is there any danger of planet Earth *actually collapsing* under the weight? I'm being hugely fanciful as usual but, looking at the concept of the literary added value of any given book in another way, what is the average amount of time a *book is actually read* during its lifespan? It must be a tiny, tiny fraction. Perhaps books should be designed to self-destruct if they remain untouched and unread for a certain number of years, in the interests of tidiness and economy of space on our overcrowded planet; a bit like biodegradable plastic bags.

Since this doesn't happen, what *does* happen to them all? Exactly nothing! They just continue to lie around in perpetuity. I'm reminded of an abandoned car I spotted in a Rome suburb a few years ago, when I was working there on a UN project. This car had just been left parked at the kerbside of a fairly major road, along which I and colleagues used to make our way in transit between our apartment hotel and the nearest local supermarket in search of cheap red wine, pasta and prosciutto. What was remarkable about the car was that its interior had been completely filled from floor to roof with books: in many cases large, leather-bound books that must have had some value when brand-new, years before, and that one would have thought would still be worth something now. But apparently not. There the car sadly sat, week after week, unbroken into by any kleptomaniac bibliophile who happened to be passing by, its enormous, heavy, dusty load weighing it down, so much that the tyres were completely flat and the chassis itself was barely shy of the level of the road. Even the municipal Roman refuse services couldn't be bothered to empty it or tow it away. Maybe it sits there still.

As for *my* collection of books, what will happen to them when I die? I can only imagine they will meet with similar treatment to those of my father's, i.e., be carted off in a tumbril to be disposed of in second-hand bookshops, at flea-markets and car boot sales. I can't imagine that very many of them will be of interest to anyone else. I have this sad vision of my (hopefully) still grieving but otherwise nonplussed children helplessly trying to offer them to this person or that, but in the end just giving them away as a job-lot to anyone willing to take them – exactly as in my father's case. Perhaps I should save them some trouble by stipulating in my will that they should be ritualistically burnt in a huge funeral pyre. If I wasn't viscerally against the concept of human cremation, I could also stipulate that my embalmed corpse should be placed on top, so the whole shooting match could be disposed of as quickly and cleanly as possible.

****

Such dreary thoughts! In the interests of returning to good cheer, here are some other fatuous books I have come across over the years:

1. *Old Father Nile*

This one I remember picking off the bookshelves of the British Council Library in Dar-es-Salaam, many years ago. Reading the blurb on the dust cover, I took it to be an account of a journey from estuary to the source of said River Nile. A modern-day equivalent, in a way, of the epic journeys of those 19th-century explorers: Speke, Burton, Baker, and the like.

So indeed it was in a sense; except that, after a couple of chapters or so describing the delights of cruising up the lower, most touristic Egyptian reaches of Luxor, Aswan etc., the author shamefacedly admitted that he and his travelling companion (aka girlfriend) had been unable to proceed any further upriver, beyond the border: due to the political situation in Sudan at the time of their journey. Didn't stop him from writing his book, however – lots of tasteful shots of the photogenic couple camping in the desert; resting at oases; going for camel rides - but very little indeed (either in the way of photographs or text) of said river. Quite bizarre really! I can only assume that the author had a contract with some publisher or other and meant to fulfil it, even if the whole point of the book had been negated by Gaafar Nimeiry, Omar al-Bashir or whichever other Sudanese president happened to be in power at the time of the epic journey.

2. *1000 Years of Annoying the French*

Or, as I would retitle it, '1000 Pages of Annoying Garbage'. A heavyweight book that Sophie gave me as a gift earlier this year, written by the ardent Francophile, (it really is difficult to tell which), Stephen Clarke. I know I have a phobia about British stereotypes of the French, but this book really does take the cake, systematically and chronologically deriding every French mishap that has occurred throughout history, and belittling every achievement. Consider the following, for example:

'The French were characteristically late for the battle... when Philippe IV got to Crécy, one of his advisers told him there was no point fighting that day, because the troops would be tired...'

'... the world-famous French cuisine... in fact, visitors (to France) found certain things lacking and had to import their own foods – and some of these proved so popular with the French that they adopted them and are convinced they invented them.'

This is a book that simply panders to all those stereotypes Brits have about the French and nothing more (vain, ineffectual, obsessed about sex...). According to the cover, Stephen Clarke has lived in France for many years and has written several other works on his pet subject: *'A Year in the Merde'; 'Ten*

Commandments for understanding the French'. etc. So, I can't believe he really has so little understanding of what his adopted country, and its inhabitants are really like. I presume he is simply writing for his audience, i.e., Daily Mail readers and their ilk, who want to go on believing what they want to believe. I suppose if it sells it must be OK. And this man has seemingly made a career of peddling this kind of stuff. Up yours, Delors!

3. *Master and Commander*, etc.

Patrick O'Brian's, *'Aubrey-Maturin'* series of novels are certainly well-written, but they irritate me greatly. Packed with detail about early 19th-century naval life: the traditions, practices, and manoeuvres, they seem to me to be written more as a vehicle for O'Brian to demonstrate how clever he is, rather than developing a story. Thus, each successive book in the series has the same ingredients: lots of incomprehensible nautical jargon, a bit of spying, a couple of naval actions (unashamedly cribbed from ones that actually took place), a bit of natural history, a bit of classical music snobbery*, a bit of philosophy, a bit of foreign and classical languages, etc., etc. They are all virtually identical, except that they are set in different locations around the world (thus giving O'Brian yet more opportunity to show off his encyclopaedic knowledge of Funchal, Port Mahon or Bridgetown as they were in

Napoleonic times, and thus further patronise the reader).
I much prefer C S Forrester's *'Hornblower'* series. They
are set in the same period, and in the same environment,
but where each book contains a well-told story, and in
which the central character - Horatio Hornblower
himself - comes across as a real person with human
foibles and weaknesses, rather than just a mouthpiece to
demonstrate the breadth and depth of the author's
scholarship.

* "...unless indeed you would prefer the Locatelli C major trio..."
"To tell you the truth, dear Commodore, I *should* prefer the Locatelli. There
is something truly dispassionate and as it were geometrical in the trio that
touches me, in something of the same manner as your paper on nutation and
the procession of the equinoxes..."

4. *Be Your Own Management Consultant*

Finally, a business book. As with *'Master of Middle
Earth',* I haven't actually read this one, but for a different
reason: I wrote it (or, to be precise, co-wrote it with a
consultant colleague), and I've never been able to
objectively read anything I've written myself. I'm not
particularly proud of it; if I remember rightly, my
colleague and I put together a proposal to a publisher
because a: we thought it would be a fun thing to do, and
b: we thought we might make some money out of it. In
fact, in both of these goals we were quite successful. Just
don't believe what is written about it on the dust cover:

> '*Be Your Own Management Consultant* puts consulting into a practical context and shows you how you can quickly acquire the skills to set up your own management consultancy and save your company a fortune in fees...'
>
> It sold reasonably well, and I have a couple of copies on my bookshelves, including editions translated into Italian *('La Consulenza Interna'),* Spanish *('Sea Su Propio Consultor Y Ahorre Dinero')* and Romanian *('Consultanta in Afaceri').* Maybe in Bucharest I'm considered to be a management guru! In fact, producing the book was little more than a good thing for the publisher, since we wrote it for nothing and received only a small percentage of the sale proceeds. I guess this kind of short-term commercial consideration is behind the publication of the majority of all books.

And so, in this roundabout way, my personal Eye of Sauron swings round again towards *'Master of Middle Earth'.*

One of several things that intrigues me about it – admittedly, based on what little of it I've actually read – is the author's view about Tolkien's other famed fantasy novel, *'The Hobbit'.* This can only be described as extreme loathing, simply because the way this earlier work is written clashes horribly with his crack-brained theories about Chains of Being, Cosmic Order and the like. As anyone who's read it will know, 'The Hobbit' is much shorter, breezier, brighter; much less loaded down with quasi-folkloric hidden meaning and possible parallels with world-changing events (industrialisation, the Cold War, the Atomic Bomb, etc.). Sometimes described merely as a children's book, it addresses such themes as the power of the ring, and the nature of evil, in a much lighter, frequently quite jocular way. So much so, that it becomes clear in MOME that Kocher wishes Tolkien hadn't written it at all:

> '...many potential readers approaching Tolkien for the first time have inferred that they must tackle *The Hobbit* first. Unfortunately, that work often puzzles, sometimes repels outright... Gandalf, the wizard of the child's story... needs nothing short of a total literary resurrection... much of this need for upgrading the characters and the plot of *The Hobbit* arises from Tolkien's treatment of them in many situations of that tale as seriocomic. He evidently believes that the children will enjoy laughing at them...'

How absurdly patronising! A bizarre case of the tail of Kocher's dog wagging the purity of Tolkien's imaginative genius!

****

As I mentioned long ago in paragraph 4, I don't have my father's original copy of MOME anymore and was obliged to buy a copy on eBay to garner my quotes for it (it cost me £2.50, with free postage). I thus (re)discovered that Paul H Kocher, (1907 – 1998) was an American academic, a highly respected figure in the world of literary criticism, 'a scholar, an author, and professor of English, having published works on Elizabethan drama, philosophy, religion and medicine'. MOME itself is generally highly rated, having undergone several reprints and been translated into different languages (not as many as BYOMC, however – touché!):

'Master of Middle Earth opens the door to a deeper and richer appreciation of Tolkien's magnificent achievement. Inside you will discover... the origin of Sauron and the nature of evil in Tolkien's universe... the Cosmology (!) of Middle Earth – is it our world at an earlier time, or does it exist in a fantastic Elsewhere?'

There is no accounting for taste, I suppose, including my own. Perhaps I should make another attempt at reading *'Master of Middle Earth'*, after all, by way of literary self-flagellation.

And Finally... Two Poems

1. Snow at York: January 25, 1974

Dry snow worries out the wind,

Forming a pregnancy of white flakes

Quivering in birth, infant-like, blind.

"And there will be rejoicing in the town,

There will be rejoicing in the town.

And sledging on the hill, and laughter.

Dark figures against the snow.

There will be rejoicing in the town."

Dry snow driven before my mind,

Awakens a boon-whiteness and a freshness;

A freshness and a fresh white wind of dawn.

2. *Turkeys*

The hard, black eye of the turkey,

Head tucked awry,

Unblinkingly cold, glinting in the pink folds

Of the neck.

Awkwardness, aloof, uneasy unkempt crown,

Challenging with forthright glare

For grain; while fleshy, three-pronged claws

Scratch the discoloured earth.

The vulture in them disappears

In smutty tufts of feathers and those scrubby claws

That span the dirt; only the bold apologetic beak and eye

Retain pin-headed, wildfowl dignity.

Eyes closed, I see them; limp, pluck-pimpled, white,

December turkeys trussed with dangling necks

In butchers' shops.

ABOUT THE AUTHOR

Kram Rednip is a former international management consultant and business writer with dual French/British nationality, who has travelled widely in the course of his professional career. He now lives quietly in France with an independent-minded wife and some cats. His good friend Clovis Buckram (who makes an appearance in the Kram Kollection) says this of him:

"Kram Rednip? Oh, he's quite a decent sort, really. Can be a bit of a wimp at times. Fancies himself as a bit of an author, with all his scratchings and scribblings. Don't see him making it onto the Booker Prize shortlist myself, but you never know, I suppose."

Booker Prize or not, the stories in the Kram Kollection reflect certain aspects of Kram's international experience, which he humbly presents in the hope they may be of interest to readers.